COWBOY'S SASSY ROOMMATE

J.P. COMEAU

🦙 I 🦙

Sadie

"No, Mommy. Please. I don't wanna!"

"Sweetheart, it's okay. It's just a little sheep. All Daddy and I want is a picture. Please, don't cry. You're a big boy, remember?"

"I'm a big boy... but I still don't want to, Mommy!"

It broke my heart to watch that sweet little boy cry against his mother's shoulder. But, what hurt even worse was watching her put her crying three-year-old on that sheep anyway. I mean, what kind of mother didn't listen to the pleas of their child when they didn't want to do something? Did they not care that he was crying his little behind off? Did they not care that he was truly scared of Barney?

"Miss? Miss!"

I drew in a deep breath. "Yes! How can I help you?"

She motioned to her son. "Could you just...help us out over here? All we want is a quick picture for his grandparents. They have pictures of all their grandchildren with animals, but unfortunately, Anthony is afraid of all of them... And we really don't know why."

Then, tell the grandparents, 'Tough stuff! The kid's scared'. "Of course. I can certainly try to help."

I walked over to the crying boy and knelt down as he clung to Barney's fluffy wool. I knew my animal was well trained and wouldn't hurt him, but his red face broke my heart.

"Hey there, what's your name?" I asked softly.

The little boy sniffled. "An-Anthony."

"Well, my name is Sadie. It's nice to meet you."

His voice fell to a hushed whisper. "Can I get off now?"

My heart broke for him. "Just one quick picture, okay? What if I stand here with you?"

He shook his head, and I looked up at his parents who were poised and ready to snap the picture.

"I don't wanna," the boy murmured.

I brushed his tears away. "If you take the picture for your parents really quickly, I've got a surprise for you."

He paused. "Surprise?"

I nodded. "Uh-huh. For all the good boys and girls. I'll give you two, just because I know you're doing this to make your parents happy. Yeah?"

He nodded slowly. "Yeah."

I brushed his cheeks off again. "All right. On my count, we're going to look at your parents and give them a massive smile. Then, it's surprise time. Ready?"

He drew in a broken breath. "O-O-O-okay. I'm ready."

I pointed to his parents, then began the countdown. "One. Two. Three! Turn and smile!"

We turned towards the camera and smiled together. And after his mother snapped a few pictures, I scooped that child off Barney's mini-saddle so quickly it would've made anyone's head spin. He clung to me, burying his face into the crook of my neck as he started crying again. And the sounds broke my heart.

I wished, with all my might, that I had the guts to tell his parents off for something like this.

"Oh! Honey, it's okay. Mommy's here. It's all done. There we go."

His mother scooped him from my arms, but my reflex to hang onto him kicked in for a split second. She shot me a deathly look, and I quickly let go of the crying boy, but I still had the urge to tell her exactly what I thought of her. Still, I put on my best face and rushed back to my stand. Ellie, my cousin, smiled and handed me two suckers from the glass container before collecting from the next child in line for a ride.

Then, I walked back up to Anthony and his parents as they continued to try and settle him down.

"Two surprises. As promised," I said.

I held the suckers out to the boy without bothering to ask

3

his parents if it was all right. Because honestly? If they were willing to go against what their little boy wanted for their bodies, then they could suck it up while I gave him a treat for dealing with their bullcrap.

I hated parents who made their kids do things they didn't want to do... over something so stupid.

Reminded me a bit of my own childhood.

Anthony sniffled. "Thank you."

I smiled. "You're very welcome. You were so brave. I'm very proud of you."

And it warmed my heart when the little boy grinned.

With the rodeo bustling around with kids and families coming from far and near to walk through my petting zoo and ride my trained sheep and goats, I crossed my arms over my chest. I drew in a sobering breath as the parents walked away with their son in their arms, and I briefly wondered if that would be me someday. I'd always wanted children. I always saw myself with a massive family; five or six kids gathered around a huge table for dinner every night. Luna, Willow, and even my cousin often got onto me about 'dreaming bigger' and 'wanting more for myself.' But, the truth of the matter was that a more traditional life appealed to me. I wanted to take care of a home. I wanted to be in a loving partnership with my husband. I wanted to bear his children.

Wasn't that the whole point of the feminist movement? Being able to choose what life we wanted for ourselves?

I don't know. The girls told me all the time I thought too much about things sometimes.

"Mommy! Look!"

Anthony's voice pulled me from my trance, and I looked in the direction of his voice. And when I saw him pointing at something, my eyes followed his movements. I saw a horse trotting up, and the boy seemed enamored by the beautiful black stallion, and I watched as his parent's faces lit up.

As the horse came closer, I noticed a lasso rope hanging from the saddle horn. The rider had probably just gotten done with the cattle roping event that was currently taking place.

"That horse. I wanna ride that horse, please?" the little boy pled.

His question tugged me towards the wooden gate that kept my animals all in one place, and I latched it behind me.

His parents marched him straight over to that horse, and my heart warmed a bit. They looked so proud that their son wanted to actually touch an animal, and I saw relief flooding their faces. Anthony put his hand against the horse and giggled as he petted it, and his father got in there to show him how to pet with the horse's coat instead of against it. His mother looked bright with pride. Or, possibly even more relief.

Either way, it taught me a good lesson in not judging people based on one incident.

I mean, it was clear that they loved their son. It was clear that they wanted only what was best for him. And all they were doing was juggling outside family expectations against the wants and wishes of their son. I couldn't blame them for that. Family always screwed things up. I knew that lesson all too well. And simply because I had caught them in a moment where grandparents trumped a kid's want, it didn't make them terrible parents.

No one is perfect.

A lesson I learned as a child from my own mother every time I found her slumped over with a needle in her arm.

Then, I saw something that made me smile. I watched that little three-year-old boy hoist his arms into the air. He kept chanting, 'Come up? Come up? Come up?' And as if he hadn't just been screaming over my sheep only a few minutes ago, I watched his parents hoist him into the arms of the rider of that beautiful, all-black stallion.

But, when my eyes fell upon who was on that saddle receiving that little boy, I froze.

"Will," I whispered.

It was none other than Will Remington. My high school sweetheart. And as he took that boy into his arms, planting him right in front of him on the saddle, my heart turned to mush. All sorts of memories came flooding back to me. The first time Will and I kissed. The night he sort of took my virginity.

The day he broke my heart and set it on fire.

What did you just learn about judging people?

I shook the thought from my head and forced my eyes away from Will. But I couldn't turn away. I watched Anthony's parents snap picture after picture of their little boy smiling brightly and naturally on top of that magnificent stallion.

I refused to look at Will, though.

His actions had not been okay. And they would never be okay. I'd never forgiven him for what he had done to me; for what he promised and failed to deliver. And I never would!

He promised me a future he then squandered while off at college. He promised me forever and then left me in his dust. I turned my back to Will, ready to put a wall between us once more. Ready to cast him to the side and not give him a second thought.

But my weakness was too much.

Before I knew it, I was peering over my shoulder and watching the scene unfold. Anthony, with his thumbs high in the sky, and Will clinging to that little boy and smiling for the world while his parents took pictures.

And when the pictures were all said and done, Will's eyes met mine once more.

...holding my gaze hostage as that cheeky little grin of his spread across his face.

2

Will

The second she peered over her shoulder, I knew I had her. Hook, line, and sinker. Just like in high school. I felt a grin spreading across my cheeks as an idea formed in my head. And finally, I had enough of Sadie's attention and the right situation to attempt damage control.

"Mister?" the little boy in front of me asked.

I peeked down at him. "How do you fancy a short ride on my horse?"

His eyes lit up, and it melted a small part of me. "Really!?"

I nodded. "If it's okay with your parents, we can go walking around a bit."

"Mom! Dad! Can I ride on the horsey with Mister!?"

I looked over at the parents as they talked among themselves, hoping and praying they said 'yes.' I felt Sadie's eyes on me as they deliberated, and I felt sweat starting to permeate the nape of my neck.

Then, the mother nodded. "As long as we walk by you, I don't see a problem with it."

The little boy threw his fists into the air. "Yeah! Let's go!"

I chuckled. "All right. Now, hold the reins like this, and I'm going to kick a bit. And once I do, Midnight will start moving. All right?"

The boy nodded. "Okay. Okay. Phew."

I grinned at his antics. "Ready?"

He nodded. "Ready."

So, I kicked Midnight softly, and off we went.

The little boy giggled with delight as I placed my hands over his. I peeked over my shoulder just long enough to see the utter shock in Sadie's eyes, and it filled me with a pride I couldn't put words to.

I'd been working for a while to prove to her that I was a different man. That I wasn't the immature teen I had been back in college. So, maybe this was the first step down a track she'd actually pay attention to.

Hopefully...

"Mom! Dad! I wanna horsey! This is awesome!" the boy exclaimed.

His father chuckled. "Well, your grandfather has those horse stables. Maybe he'll let you take care of one of his horses."

The boy went to raise his fists. "Yeah!"

I caught his movements before he tugged on the reins. "Whoa, whoa, whoa. Gotta be careful with those in your hands. Raise them up too much, and Midnight will stop walking! Don't wanna do that now, do we?"

The little boy shook his head. "No, Mister. We don't."

I smiled. "All right. We'll do one walk around the smaller parking lot before it's time for some lemonade. It's a hot one out here today. You're gonna need fluids."

His mother hummed. "Mmmm sounds so good right now."

And his father took the cue. "I'll go get us some and meet you at the stopping point. Where are y'all headed?"

I pointed. "Right to the lemonade stand, actually. Figured I'd get one myself. See you over there?"

The father smiled. "See you over there."

He kissed his wife softly before trotting off, and I found myself a bit jealous. Not that I wanted his wife or anything like that. I mean, I had my own reputation, but I didn't hook up with women that were taken. Not my kinda style. Still, though, having someone to kiss like that? Even quickly, before heading out somewhere?

I'd been craving that in my life for a while now.

Seeing Sadie more and more at the rodeos and around town had me thinking a lot about the good ole' days. The days where I'd walk over to her place with half-melted ice cream, and we'd sit on the porch, cuddling, while we ate. The days where I came home from college for a weekend on a whim and surprised her with flowers and a great, big kiss.

I missed those days with her.

Part of me even wanted those days back.

Still, her business was taking off, and I was proud of her for that. Sadie had always enjoyed animals, it was one of the things that bonded us when we met back in high school. I remembered how she cried with she tried to rescue a baby squirrel who had fallen from its nest and died a few days later. Sadie's love of animals and my love of rodeos had threaded themselves together like bread and butter, and it blossomed a relationship between the two of us that lasted almost three solid years.

Until my bullshit antics got me into trouble.

As I rode with that little boy in my lap, my mind reminisced. I remembered back to all of the talks Sadie and I had about our futures. What we wanted to do. Why we wanted to go off to college. Dreams and aspirations and life goals for ourselves. I knew she desperately wanted to work with animals, but she never had the stomach Willow or Luna possessed. I knew she couldn't stomach the idea of being a veterinarian, or a vet tech. So, when her brilliant little plan of offering the kids at the rodeo a petting zoo and animals to ride that were their size started popping up every weekend, I couldn't help but smile.

Though, today was the first day she'd caught me smiling at her.

And I didn't want it to stop.

Even back when we were kids, Sadie had always been tenacious. Always looking for a way to get what she wanted without abiding by all of the rules everyone else did. It was one of the many things that made me fall in love with her. It was one of the many reasons why I asked her out when we were nothing but sophomores in high school.

It was also one of the many reasons why I'd been dreaming of getting her back.

You were such an idiot back then, Will.

I pulled myself out of my thoughts and focused back on the horse ride. I held the little boy steady as we rode off towards the lemonade stand, and I still felt Sadie's eyes boring a hole in the back of my head. Her glistening eyes locking with mine only made me miss her more, though. That girl had been the only one for me, and I screwed things up when I promised her the world and gave her nothing but a slap in the face. I had been an idiot back then—an arrogant, eccentric, selfish idiot.

Not anymore, though.

I just had to prove that to Sadie now that I had her attention.

After breaking Sadie's heart and not being able to win her back, I made a decision about my life. I told myself I'd never get so deeply involved with a woman like that ever again. Mostly because I had been a teenager at the time and wanted to do nothing but have fun. I wanted my selfish cake, and I wanted to eat as much of it as I could. And during college, that sufficed. My business degree flew by, and despite the partying I did, I received A's and B's during my entire tenure.

But when I graduated? I had been lost.

Until Mom and Dad handed my brothers and me the petroleum company.

The truth of the matter was I didn't want anyone in my life getting hurt while I was partying. I didn't want to take on yet another person I could fall in love with and then hurt them with my actions. If I was going to party, everyone else had to stay at arm's length so my partying wouldn't hurt them. At the time, it was the only solution my asshole nineteen-year-old brain could come up with.

Probably one of the reasons why my attempts to win Sadie back were half-assed, at best.

You're doing it again. Focus on the present, not on the past.

"Lemonade!" the little boy exclaimed.

I felt him wiggling around in my grasp before he released the reins.

"Whoa, whoa, whoa. Slow down there, buddy. Here. Let me help," I said.

I brought Midnight to a halt and handed the small boy back to his mother. And when they turned around, there was Dad, holding a small lemonade for their three-year-old and a large one with two straws. The pang of jealousy grew in my gut as a petite teenage girl with heart eyes stamped onto her face came up to me with a medium lemonade all my own.

"Here you go, Will," she said with a giggle.

I simply nodded and took the lemonade, trying not to give

her anymore to go on. Teenagers tripped over themselves nowadays when it came to 'older men' like myself and Bryce. Or even Bart, despite the fact that my younger brother's profession was a bit... dull. Possibly even comedic.

I mean, who the hell aspired to be a geologist when they grew up? Unless your father had become a billionaire from the massive oil patch under the Rocking R Ranch.

Either way, after I took a long pull from my lemonade, I waved to the little boy and turned Midnight around. After winning first place in all my events, I needed to get ready to head back to the ranch. Plus, I was aching to see the look on Sadie's face. Would she look surprised? Shocked? Proud? Maybe she'd have those same heart eyes stamped onto her face like the teenage girl who kept giggling next to my leg.

"You're a great rider, Mr. Will," she said.

I nodded mindlessly. "I appreciate that. And thanks for the lemonade."

A gruff voice sounded. "That'll be five bucks."

I slowly looked over and saw a very stout and tall man looming over the teenage girl. A good father, if I did say so myself. I dug around in my pocket before the little boy's father interjected, handing the massive mountain of a man a five-dollar bill on my behalf.

"Here you go," the father said before he looked up at me, "and thank you for my son's horse ride. Really. He'll be talking about it for weeks."

I grinned. "It's the least I can do. Thank you for the lemonade."

After finally getting myself out of that weird-ass exchange, I reined my mount around. But, when my eyes scanned the edge of the parking lot for Sadie, she was nowhere to be found. I saw her animals and another woman I recognized as Sadie's cousin Ellie tending to the venue. I saw parents taking pictures and swatting at their children's hands when they were too rough with the animals. But, Sadie? With her brown eyes with green speckles that reminded me of the forest that surrounded my home?

They were nowhere.

And it tore my heart to shreds.

"Come on, Midnight. Let's get you some water and some oats," I murmured.

I kicked his sides and clicked my tongue, riding off with one hand gripping the reins. I sipped my lemonade as we trotted back behind the arena towards the Rocking R Ranch trailer that we used both as transportation and advertisement. Then, I hopped down, finished my lemonade, and started going through the process of loading up Midnight to go home.

Before I pulled out my phone to text my brothers.

Me: Bryce. Bart. I need to talk. Beers at my cabin? Say, around six? I'll grill out some steaks for us.

Then, I shoved my phone back into my pocket and hopped into my truck. Ready to head home, wash Midnight down, and settle into an evening spent with my two brothers.

Maybe they could shake me from the trance Sadie blanketed over my mind.

3

Sadie

Willow stood. "Finally! The woman of the hour arrives."

I smiled. "I'm hardly the woman of the hour."

Luna embraced me in a tight hug. "I'm sorry, but I thought you were the one that called us because you had your highest-grossing day at the rodeo ever."

I giggled. "Okay, okay, maybe I'm a little bit 'the woman of the hour.'"

Willow interjected. "Hey, I want a hug, too. Now that I don't have a baby attached to my boob."

I hugged her, as well. "Not our fault. You wanted to get pregnant. You know you did."

"Yep, I can't deny it. Just happened sooner than I had expected." Willow smirked.

The three of us embraced and giggled before we sat down for lunch at a local cafe. Yesterday at the rodeo had been my best day, monetarily, and I wanted to celebrate with the two girls that encouraged me to start this business in the first place. Cafe De La May was my favorite place to eat in this town. They had the best homemade desserts, and their bowls of soup were legitimate bowls, like at grandma's house. Coupled with a few slices of toasted bread and their creamy butter and I was in heaven every single time.

"So, Luna. How's your father doing after his surgery?" I asked as I sat down.

She flopped into her chair, sighing. "Bitching, like always. We all tried to prepare him for how rough this recovery would be. But, it seems like no amount of prepping can prepare someone for something like health issues."

Willow furrowed her brow. "Things okay at the house? You need any help or anything?"

Luna shrugged. "If you've got access to chloroform so I can douse him every time he tries to argue with me, then sure. I could use some help."

I threw my head back with laughter. "Well, we all know your father's a stubborn old man. It doesn't shock me that he's fighting you every step of the way."

Willow took her hand. "Seriously, Luna. Whatever you need, we're there for you. Okay?"

Luna drew in a curt breath. "Well, right now isn't about me. It's about Sadie and this budding business of hers!"

All eyes were on me as I placed my order with the waitress.

"Sorry, about that," I said as my attention returned to them, "what's going on?"

Willow shoved me playfully. "We're only trying to admire your business acumen."

Luna sipped her water. "Yeah, you said you netted--what?-- three grand yesterday?"

I nodded. "And even after taking out expenses, and giving a couple hundred to Ellie before she drove back to Dallas. It still puts two grand in the bank."

Willow rubbed my back. "That's amazing. I'm really happy for you."

Luna smiled. "Me, too. We know how much you've wanted to work with a miniature menagerie for a while now."

I leaned back. "I told you guys I'd find a way. I just needed to find my own way."

Willow giggled. "Honestly? I'm just glad you're not working at that grocery store anymore. You were miserable there."

Luna snickered. "Yeah, and miserable to be around because of it."

I shot her a look. "Hey. Not my fault that damn manager was a bit too handsy all the time."

Willow folded her arms over her chest. "I still think you should have reported the dickweed."

I sighed. "Well, I didn't want to burn a bridge just in case this petting zoo rodeo idea of mine didn't take off, and I needed my job back."

Luna kicked me softly under the table. "Man, look at you, being all adult and shit."

I smiled at her. "Yeah, when are you going to join the fold?"

Willow hopped on the banter bandwagon. "She's got a point. I mean, I'm with Bryce, and we've got a family. I got a house I'm holding down."

I nodded. "And I've got my business that's officially paying bills."

Luna licked her lips. "Well, when I'm ready to grow up, I will. But, in the meantime? I'm still the one having fun while you two are the ones strapped with responsibility and boredom."

Willow grinned deviously. "Trust me, time at home is anything but boring."

I puckered my lips. "Ooooo, girl! I want details."

Luna wiggled her eyebrows. "All of the lovely details."

The three of us giggled as my food touched down in front of me, and then we all jumped in. Luna chomped on her sandwich while Willow sucked down her salad. And me? Well, I couldn't dip my bread into that tomato bisque any quicker. The three of us devoured our food in complete silence before ordering one of their massive desserts to split between the three of us.

Then, we dove back into the conversation.

"Anyway," Willow said, "how's that house treating you?"

Luna patted her lips with the napkin. "Yeah, you still got enough space in that tiny little thing?"

I giggled. "You know I've never needed a lot of space, guys."

Willow snickered. "Yeah, well, when your animals have more room in the barn than you do in the house? There might be a priority issue swimming around in there somewhere."

Luna pointed her fork at me. "She's got a point. That little two-bedroom-one-bathroom thing you rent with all that space out back can't possibly be doing you any favors."

Willow hopped back in. "And I'm sure it's the reason you eat out so much. I mean, come on. That kitchen? Not even one person could cook a whole meal in it!"

I shook my head. "It's plenty of space for just me. And besides, I'm only one person. I've got sixteen animals that need space to roam and play and train. So, yeah, sixteen-to-one gets more of the space every time, no matter where I am."

Luna scoffed. "Don't you want to bring a guy over sometimes, though?"

Willow licked her lips. "Lord knows you don't get out enough."

I blinked. "Uh, thanks? Maybe? And no, I don't want to bring a guy over. Men are the last thing from my mind right now. Right now? My focus is on scaling my business... trying to make it profitable during the off-seasons when it comes to the rodeo. Can't be making money only seven months out of the year. That won't keep me afloat, no matter how much I rake in."

Luna shrugged. "Well, why don't you buy your own place with your own land and put your animals on it and open up a petting zoo right there on your property for people to come see?"

Willow pointed with her fork. "That's actually not a bad idea."

"How much do you have socked away?" Luna butted in.

"Please tell me you got that savings account up and running like I told you to." Willow smacked her lips.

"Oh! What about the donations you got in order to start this thing in the first place? Did you use all of it up getting started?"

I held up my hand. "Can we stop with the barrage of questions for a second? Our dessert is coming."

When the waitress set the massive slice of chocolate cake with ice cream in the middle of us, we ceased to talk. And the silence was refreshing. I knew they meant well and wanted what was best for me. But, sometimes my two best friends were a bit too much to handle. I mean, I was the quiet one of the bunch. The introverted one. The 'different' one, for lack of a better term. So, it was usually Willow and Luna against myself when it came to any issue.

Including the issue of my business and living space, apparently.

Luna piped up again. "If you don't like the petting zoo on your property idea, then maybe you could take a part-time gig somewhere and then just request off on the weekends when you've got the rodeo?"

I shook my head. "I still have to train my little gals and guys, which is what I do during the week."

Willow took a massive bite of ice cream. "Maybe you could get more of a variety, like add peacocks and different kinds of chickens. Make it a learning experience about where eggs come from. Or something like that. Then, you know... do your own advertising? Maybe draw families that aren't usually rodeo lovers out to the rodeo grounds just to take their kids to your awesome venue... or what ever you call it?"

I snickered. "You mean Sadie's Menagerie. That's the name on my awesome banner I'm having made. It'll be done in a few weeks?"

Willow held up her finger as she struggled through her brain freeze, which made me giggle.

"Might want to re-think an entire spoonful of it next time."

Luna giggled with me. "She's right. Maybe not so big of a bite next time, Willow."

She glared at both of us. "Hey, just because I like ice cream doesn't mean I have to be shamed for it."

I held up my hands. "No one's shaming you for anything, crazy. Just trying to prevent another brain freeze."

Willow picked up another spoonful. "Just let it hurt. Because it hurts so good."

She took another massive bite before it flung her head-first into another brain freeze, which made Luna and I fall apart in laughter. Willow had always been a glutton for good food, which made her the best person to go out to eat with. She always knew the best spots and the names of all the hole-in-the-wall places that us locals hadn't even discovered yet.

But, even with a mouthful of cake, the one thing that had been heavy on my mind since yesterday came blurting out.

"So, I saw Will at the rodeo."

The girls both looked at me with quizzical stares as I swallowed down the rich chocolate.

"Doesn't shock me," Willow said, "he and Bryce were working around the clock this past week to get Midnight ready for the cattle roping competition."

Luna leaned back. "And I heard Bart came back into town to compete in steer wrestling."

Willow gasped. "Really?! Bart's in town? Since when?"

Luna turned her attention away from me. "Apparently, since Tuesday. He drove home at the drop of a hat when Bryce asked."

Willow furrowed her brow. "How did I not know this?"

I wrinkled my nose. "The question is, how do you know all of this, Luna? About Bart?"

She shrugged. "I hear things."

I blinked. "Uh-huh."

Willow leaned forward. "I've got a kid with Bryce, and I didn't know about this, but somehow you do, and you don't even come by the ranch on a regular basis?"

I grinned delightfully. "I smell a secret."

Luna turned things around on me. "Says the woman who's apparently been dwelling on seeing her ex since yesterday."

Willow whipped her head toward me. "That's right! You said you saw Will. Why would you bring that up?"

I rolled my eyes. "It was just an update. He gave one of the boys at my petting zoo a small horse ride, and it was just one of those things, you know?"

Willow grinned. "This time was different, wasn't it?"

I scoffed. "What?"

Luna abandoned her chocolate-covered fork. "She's right. You've got a little sparkle in your eye."

"My eyes aren't sparkling, you ninny."

Willow snapped her fingers. "You only insult people when you feel backed into a corner."

"Why do you feel backed into a corner, Sadie?"

I narrowed my eyes. "Why don't you stop coming at me so much, Luna?"

Willow settled her hand on top of mine. "What happened with Will, Sadie?"

Luna nodded. "You can be honest with us. We're picking with you, but we won't judge you?"

She squeezed my hand. "It was different this time, wasn't it?"

Luna started making soft kissy faces, and I wanted to smack the look right off her face.

Uh oh, I do feel cornered.

I felt my cheeks blushing before I even tried to speak my piece, and even I knew something was different. That something had changed. I didn't want it to happen, either. I didn't want things to be different. I wanted to keep hating Will for what he'd done to me for the rest of my life. It made things easier that way.

"Sadie, talk to us," Willow said.

I pulled my hand away from hers. "All right, look. Even if things were different when I saw him yesterday, it doesn't change what he did. It doesn't change the fact that he cheated and still hasn't apologized for it."

Luna blinked. "Wait, what?"

Willow furrowed her brow tightly. "You said he apologized when he came to see you. That was a long time ago."

I sighed. "I lied, okay? I just--everyone was upset, and everything was so confusing--."

Luna slid forward in her seat. "So, when he came to see you after you found those pictures on Instagram of him kissing other girls at some bullshit party, what did he actually do?"

I swallowed hard, remembering it all in a flash. "He brought flowers and chocolates and tried to convince me that it was just a one-time thing and wouldn't happen again."

Willow scoffed. "That pompous, arrogant little--."

Luna drew in a sharp breath. "So, he never apologized for kissing that other girl."

I shook my head. "Gave me every excuse under the sun, but no apology. 'She was drunk,' 'I was drunk,' 'everyone was drunk,' 'I don't remember it'..."

Willow shook her head. "You deserve better than him. You know that, right?"

I shrugged. "What if something inside me is telling me something else?"

Luna pinned me with a look. "Do you still love him?"

Silence fell over the table, and I wanted to melt into absolute nothingness. Because I knew the answer. I knew the answer, and I was ashamed to say it.

"Sadie?" Willow asked softly.

I sighed. "I'll always love Will, in a way."

Luna kept on. "But do you love him now? I mean, really love him... not just as a high school crush kind of love?"

I shrugged. "I don't know, okay!? I just--."

I pinched the bridge of my nose as I sighed heavily.

"I just--he was my first everything, you know? First date. First kiss. The first man that ever gave me an orgasm, though we never actually had sex. I thought it was always so romantic that he never pushed me into that kind of thing. That he was willing to wait until I was ready."

Willow started massaging my shoulder. "Just never felt right?"

I leaned my head back. "No, it's never felt right with any guy. I mean, if anything? It felt more right with Will than anyone else, though it never felt right enough to act on. If that makes any sense."

Luna snickered. "I'm just proud of you for always sticking to your guns and not fucking around with every guy that comes along."

I giggled bitterly. "Like I even entertain guys like that."

Willow's hand slid down my arm. "Begs the question as to why you've never really dated after Will, though."

Luna hopped in. "Which brings us back to our original question: are you still in love with Will?"

And as my head sat upright on my shoulders, my eyes volleying between my two best friends, I realized something.

I had absolutely no idea how in the world to answer that question.

4

Will

"You know, you've really made this little spot out here homey," Bart said.

I cracked open a beer and handed it to Bryce. "I keep that pond out there stocked, too, in case you wanna fish while you're here."

Bryce furrowed his brow. "I didn't know you kept it stocked. Why can't I come fish?"

I plopped down onto the porch swing. "Because it's mine. I've got a three-bedroom, two-bathroom cabin with one lake and five acres of hunting space. You've got everything else. Go fish in your own lake."

Bryce pouted. "But it's so far away."

I shrugged. "Tough tits, big brother."

Bart chuckled. "I appreciate the offer, and I might just take you up on it if I've got time."

Bryce sipped his beer. "The garden out back looks good, too. Saw it when I was driving up."

Bart thumbed over his shoulder. "What you got out there? Tomatoes? Beans?"

I nodded. "Mhm. And cabbage. Lettuce. Spinach. Also? Carrots and tomatoes."

Bart grinned. "Well, aren't you just livin' off the land out here."

I snickered. "You know that's what I've always wanted to do. Go into town for the rodeos, and spend the rest of my time here."

Bryce tipped back the rest of his beer. "When he's not at the office."

I pointed over my head. "Which is only a half a mile that way. So close, I can walk it every morning and evening."

Bryce leaned over to Bart. "Which means he's smelling ripe when he gets into the office."

Bart chuckled as I threw back the rest of my beer. "Hey, at least I take a shower when I get there. Besides, it's nice to get away from the hustle and bustle. College and city life at the University of Texas while I was there was much, much too busy for me."

Bart polished off his beer. "Those college frat parties too wild for you?"

A pang of hurt slapped me across the face. "More like, they took too much from me."

Silence blanketed my front porch as I reached into the cooler for another beer.

"So, we wanna run down what happened at the rodeo?" Bryce asked.

Bart leaned back, stretching his legs out. "Actually, I'd like to hear about this little rumor I heard."

My eyes met his. "What rumor?"

He grinned. "I heard you gave some boy a ride on Midnight after your competition?"

Bryce paused. "Wait, what?"

Relief washed through my veins. "Oh, yeah. That. I don't know, he was crying and snotting everywhere, but he liked the horse, so I let him get up there with me."

Bart snickered. "And you just happened to give him a ride while he was up there?"

I shrugged. "What? What's so bad about it?"

Bryce shook his head. "Not bad. Just... out of character."

I scoffed. "What the hell does that mean?"

Bart chuckled. "It means you're shit with kids, so it's shocking to us that you'd willingly deal with a kid out of the goodness of your own heart."

I rolled my eyes. "I don't hate kids, y'all. I just think they're bratty little shits whose parents spoil them too much."

Bryce sighed. "Well, usually you're ranting about how the rodeo is no place for kids. How it's dangerous and shit like that."

Bart paused. "Wait, wait, wait! I know it. I've got it."

I blinked. "Got what?"

He pointed at me. "The reason why you did it."

I stood. "Why the hell is it so hard to believe that I just wanted to do something nice for someone?"

Bart smiled up at me. "There was a woman involved, wasn't there?"

Bryce licked his lips. "How the hell did I not pin that down sooner?"

My jaw dropped to the floor. "You guys think it takes some girl batting her eyelashes at me to do something nice for some kid? Seriously?"

Bart shrugged. "Hey, all we know is what you show us."

Bryce reached for another beer. "And in the past? That's all you've shown us."

"Or anyone else, for that matter."

Their words struck a chord with me, and it hurt. "Well, there were multiple women staring at me yesterday, in case you were curious. Hot women, too."

Bart barked with laughter. "So, you're going to start being philanthropic with your horse and your time just to get laid by all these hot women?"

I pointed at him. "Sadie's better than that, and you know it."

The second the words flew out of my mouth; everything around me fell silent. Even the forest around my cabin seemed to hold its breath. Shit. I had really stepped in it. And as I distracted myself with chugging my beer, I heard my brothers scooting their chairs closer to the porch swing.

Closer to me.

"Don't do that," I said.

Bryce stopped moving. "Do what?"

I pointed at his chair. "Get all close like that, like we're at a pow-wow."

Bart shrugged. "Just trying to be there for you."

I tossed my second beer bottle into the trash can on the porch. "Well, you can stop it. Nothing's wrong."

Bryce paused. "What happened between you two, anyway?"

Bart crossed his ankles. "Yeah, you never really did tell us what happened. Just that you were at a party, came home, had a fight, and broke up."

I took off my Stetson, plopped it down beside me on the swing and raked my fingers through my hair. "And I don't want to talk about it now."

Bryce clicked his tongue. "You met another girl at that party, didn't you?"

I eased myself back onto the porch swing. "Do we really have to do this?"

Bryce sucked air through his teeth. "Simple yes or no question there, Will."

I slid my hands down my face. "Yes, I kissed another girl at that party."

Bart hissed. "Jesus, Will."

I held my hands out. "Look, we were both drunk. It was my first frat party. I regretted it the second it happened. I came home with flowers and candy to try and make things up to Sadie, but she wasn't having it."

Bart sighed. "Did you apologize?"

I blinked. "What?"

Bryce chuckled bitterly. "So, you show up with gifts, don't apologize, and expect the girl you cheated on to forgive you?"

I growled. "I didn't cheat. I just kissed the girl."

Bart nodded. "You kissed someone who wasn't your girl-friend of almost three years. That's the definition of cheating."

"Fine, I cheated! Okay!?"

Birds cawed in the distance, and a rabbit scurried about as my voice echoed off the corners of the forestry around me.

"I cheated, and I tried to make it right, but she wouldn't let me, okay?" I rattled off quickly. "And she had every right to do so."

Bryce reached for my hand. "At least you acknowledge that."

I leaned away from him. "Yeah, don't touch me."

Bart held up his hands. "No touching. Got it."

Bryce shook his head. "Why the hell didn't you tell us about this sooner?"

I scoffed. "What the hell would it have changed? Talking about it wouldn't have brought Sadie back to me."

Bart leveled his eyes with my face. "It might not have turned you into such a closed-off, angry person, though. Had you just talked."

I chewed on the inside of my cheek. "Whatever. If you guys really think all of this bullshit has to do with some apology I did or didn't give all those years ago, then you're idiots. And just to prove you wrong, I'm going to start doing nicer things for people from now on. Whether or not someone is watching me do it. Because for me? Seeing the smile on that boy's face was worth it. It made me feel good, and I deserve that."

Bryce nodded. "That's good. It's a good place to start."

Bart stifled a chuckle. "Bet all those hot women staring at you didn't hurt that heady feeling, though, huh?"

While Bryce and Bart took shots at my expense, I retreated inside of my head. I wasn't just a playboy like everyone thought. There was more to me. Always had been.

At least, I wanted there to be more to me.

Maybe that's why Sadie left. Because she knew you were too shallow for her.

"I'm not shallow," I murmured.

Bryce stopped laughing. "What was that?"

I stood to my feet. "I'm not shallow. I'm not this asshole everyone thinks I am. And I'm going to prove it to all of you."

Bart held up his hands in mock surrender. "Hey, we're your brothers. We love you, no matter who you are."

And just as I went to rebuttal, my phone started vibrating in my pocket. So, I rummaged around until I found it and pulled it out.

Only to see Willow calling me.

"Well, I guess the girls have been talking," I said.

Bart paused. "Why do you say that?"

I turned the phone around. "Because Willow's calling me right now."

Bryce jammed his hand into his pocket. "I wonder if she tried me first."

I shook my head. "Doubt it."

"Hopefully it's not an emergency."

But when he checked his phone, he saw he didn't have a missed call from Willow. Or even as much as a text. She was calling me, and only me.

So, Bart stood to his feet. "Well, I think it's time for me to get going, Bryce?"

I answered the phone. "See you guys later. I'm gonna go take this call."

As I backtracked into my cabin, I held the phone to my ear, ignoring the curious glances of my brothers as they made their way off my porch and into the night.

"Willow! Hey. What's up? Everything all right?"

I just hoped that talking to the girls hadn't done any more damage.

It was clear to me that I'd already done enough of that.

5

Sadie

I picked up Willow's phone call as I fell onto my couch. "Hey girl, what's up?"

She yawned in my ear. "I'd love to chat, but I gotta make it quick. I'm exhausted from today."

I furrowed my brow. "Everything okay?"

"Oh, yeah, yeah," she said with another yawn, "I just wanted to call really quickly and invite you to come out to the ranch."

I paused. "Uh, sure? I mean, is there a specific reason?"

"Eh, nothing really special. Bryce and I figured we could get everyone together tomorrow since it's gonna be a slow--."

She yawned in my ear, and this time I joined her.

"You can't do that," I said.

She snickered tiredly. "Bryce wants to do a cookout after training tomorrow, and I figured everyone could come out and hang out before we start cooking and stuff. That's all."

"Luna's going?"

"Yep. Bart, Bryce, and Will are already in. Just needing to know if you're coming, too."

I sighed. "I mean, it sounds like it's going to be fun. I've never been invited to the practice arena before. Should I bring something with me for the cookout?"

"Nah. I've got it covered with side dishes. Just bring your own alcohol if you want it."

"Is there a special occasion going on or something?"

"No. Why do you ask?"

I shrugged. "I don't know. Just never been invited out to the ranch during working hours, and suddenly we're all coming out for a day?"

"I mean, you don't have to come if you don't want to. It started out as 'just a brothers' sort of thing, then Bryce asked me if you girls wanted to come, so I'm just calling to ask."

"Well, I think it sounds like fun. Count me in."

"Great. All you have to do is show up around noon with your own alcohol, and we'll do the rest. See you tomorrow, girl!"

I smiled. "See you then. Love you."

"Love you, too."

I fell asleep on the couch that evening with all sorts of questions running through my mind. And when I got up that morning, I was no closer to any answers. A cookout? At the practice ranch? The last time I wanted to visit the ranch, Bryce gave some massive spiel about how a workspace was a workplace and not a place to fraternize. So, all of a sudden, we were having a cookout there?

Something wasn't right.

"Time to get ready," I said with a grunt.

I heaved myself off the couch and cleaned myself up before grabbing some wine from the fridge door. I wasn't a heavy drinker, never had been. But, I enjoyed a glass of wine or two every now and again. And after taking stock of myself in the mirror, I gathered my things and headed for the ranch.

Where I quickly got sucked into playing with Willow's baby girl.

"Oh, my goodness. Hello there, you cutie pie. Yes, you're the cutest. Yes, you are. Yes, yes, yes, you are."

The little one cooed up at me and blew a spit bubble that popped and made her laugh. Which made me smile even brighter. After hugging Willow's neck and quickly scooping her nine-month-old out of her arms, I felt someone take my bottle of wine and whisk it away somewhere. Where it went, I didn't have a clue. But I also didn't care.

Not when Ariel's eyes were staring back at me.

"You have your mommy's eyes. Yes, you do. And they are the prettiest," I said softly.

"Fancy seeing you here."

The second I heard Will's voice, I stopped bouncing the little child in my arms. How in the world had I forgotten so quickly that *all* of the brothers were going to be at this thing?

I felt warmth creep up my spine. I slowly turned around with Ariel in my arms, and I watched Will's eyes drop to the child.

"Well, here's where you went, Ariel. Yes, is Auntie Sadie treating you well? Is she? You can tell me if she isn't. You can tattletail all you want with me."

I stared at him as if he'd grown himself a fourth head.

I thought Will hated kids.

He held his arms out for her, and I wasn't sure what possessed me to hand Ariel over, but I did. And when I saw the smile that crossed Will's face, I felt something in my ovaries kick into gear. When we were teenagers, all Will talked about was running his parent's company, traveling all over the world, and never having kids. He had always been adamant about that, and I loved him so much that it was something I was willing to compromise about my own life in order to keep him in it.

So, seeing him with Willow and Bryce's little girl in his arms filled a hole in my soul I had forgotten ever formed in the first place.

But, it all ended much too soon because the second Will handed her back to me, my attention fell to Ariel once more. I smiled down at the beautiful baby girl who was about ready to fall asleep, and I started rocking side to side as softly as I could.

Until Will's cheeky grin caught the corner of my eye.

"What?" I asked, not bothering to look over at him.

"Wasn't that your cousin Ellie I saw helping you at the rodeo?"

I nodded my head. "Yes, she had the weekend off. She's training to be a farrier in Dallas."

"That's awesome. I've never met a female blacksmith."

"Yes. I'm very proud of her. She will be looking for work in a few months."

Will took another step, closing the distance between us. "What really matters, though, is how I noticed you couldn't get enough of me at the rodeo, huh?"

I rolled my eyes. "Whatever you need to tell yourself, Will. Oh, yes. Whatever he needs to tell himself, right?"

I tickled the small child's cheek before her eyes fell closed for good. But, Will's chuckle pulled me from the trance this small bundle of joy put me in.

"Well, I'm about to start practicing myself, if you'd like to watch."

I turned my back to him. "I think I'll go lay this bundle of joy down somewhere. Don't get trampled."

I heard him chuckling as I walked away, and I went in search of a playpen. Surely, they had one out here somewhere in one of these rooms. I ducked into all of them, finding nothing but office desks and dimly-lit lamps and terrible decor choices by whoever dwelled in these offices on a regular basis. But, once I couldn't find a place for a sleeping baby, I resigned myself to holding Ariel while she slept.

And I hated how much I had to work to not stare at Will.

Seeing him practicing high on his horse kept me intrigued. Between the sweat dripping down his brow and the curt commands he gave to his horses, I kept staring even though I didn't want to. I studied him as he rode by, fully concentrating on what he was doing. His arms, sweating from exertion. His legs, flexing every time he eased himself off the saddle to ride through a gallop. The veins in his neck, popping from his intense concentration.

I mean, Will had always been sexy to me. But, this was an entirely different level of heat I'd never experienced with him. Now that we were grown and out in the world trying to pave our way, he was more of a man than any other person I'd ever come across. Or even attempted to date, for that matter. No longer was he the boy that broke my heart. No longer was he the mindless frat boy who only cared about drinking and scoring with the ladies.

Oh, no. Will was a man. A career-holding, horse-training, rodeo-competing man.

With the muscles to boot.

"Aww, there's my little girl. She getting comfy with Aunt Sadie?"

I whipped around at the sound of Willow's voice. "She's been asleep for about half an hour or so now."

Willow held out her arms. "Here. I can go put her down in her crib. Maria, my housekeeper, is at the house, so it'll give us girls a couple of good hours to talk and maybe have a glass of wine?"

I handed her child back to her. "Sounds good to me. Point me in the direction where I can get some glasses started."

Luna made her way to us. "I heard 'glasses' and figured wine was now involved."

I looked over at her. "I figured I would've seen you by now. Did you just get here?"

Luna blushed. "Yes, and no."

Willow giggled. "Sounds like a story to be told over wine."

Luna linked her arm in mine. "Which is why we're going to go find the wine. Care to come on an adventure with me?"

I narrowed my eyes playfully. "You were with a guy, weren't you?"

She rolled her eyes. "Like I haven't watched you drool over Will for the past thirty minutes."

My jaw fell open. "I was not. I was simply--."

Willow snickered. "Yeah, yeah, yeah. I'll be back in a few minutes. Save the juicy gossip for me, would you?"

However, once Willow turned to walk away with Ariel to put her down for a nap, I felt someone staring at us. I felt someone studying us. So, I turned with Luna to see who was watching.

And caught Luna waving softly at Bart as he walked by.

❧ 6 ❧

Will

I had to focus much too hard on training in order to get it done. Mostly because I felt Sadie staring at me the entire time. No matter how much she fought it, I knew she'd never be able to resist watching me.

The issue was that I wanted to watch her, as well.

I got my chance, though, once training wrapped up and the cookout started. The girls were already two glasses of wine in each, and they were giggling off in a corner while Bryce and I manned the grill. And Bart? Well, he kept going over to the girls and refilling their glasses with bottles of wine from Bryce's wine cellar.

And I noticed his eyes heavily on Luna.

"There something going on between those two?" I asked.

Bryce flipped the burgers. "Who?"

"Luna and Bart."

"Oh, yeah. Saw them talking outside by his truck a little while ago. They looked pretty chummy."

I grinned. "You think he's got the hots for her?"

He shrugged. "What else could it be? I've never seen Bart with anything but a glass of whiskey or a beer in his hands. And now he's refilling wine glasses?"

I crossed my arms over my chest. "You make a solid point."

"Who's the older man with her, though?"

I felt Bryce's eyes on me. "Are you kidding?"

I looked over at him. "What?"

"The older man with Luna? That's David, you dumbass. Her father."

I blinked. "Oh."

"Yeah. She's her father's caretaker, you know."

"Wait, I didn't know that. Since when?"

He sighed. "Since all of his rodeo-riding and bronco-bucking days caught up with him. The man's riddled with arthritis. And Willow told me her father's staring down the barrel of a double-hip replacement just to keep the future pain under control."

"Oh, yikes."

"Yep."

"That sucks."

"Really does."

I watched Sadie, and the girls throw their heads back in

laughter at something, and the sound seized my heart. With a massive smile across her face and her hair wild from the humidity of the day, she looked just as beautiful as the first day I ever laid eyes on her back when I was a sophomore in high school. I wiped the sweat from my brow as my pelvis began to heat. My heart kicked into overdrive, pumping wildly in my chest. It wasn't until I felt a slap against my pec that I ripped myself away from my own trance.

And saw Bart grinning at me.

"What?" I asked.

He grinned. "Don't let her catch you staring. Not a good look, Will."

I scoffed. "Like you haven't snuck a glance or two at Luna."

Bryce pointed at Bart with his tongs. "You want a slice of that? You'll have to make friends with her father. Might as well use the opportunity."

Bart nodded. "Yeah, he and I were actually talking. Apparently, Luna quit her job at a shop of some sort to take care of him full-time. Did you guys know that?"

I shook my head. "I didn't know."

Bryce nodded. "I did, though."

I furrowed my brow. "How did you know?"

Bart chuckled. "I mean, it's not like he lives with and has had a kid with one of her best friends."

I clicked my tongue. "Point taken."

Bryce snickered. "The two of you have it bad. So, why don't you guys just do something about it?"

I shook my head. "I don't have shit bad. That's not my thing."

Bart nudged me. "Yeah, well, you said kids weren't your thing. But, you're the one volunteering to babysit more than anyone else, am I right?"

I held my hands up in mock surrender. "Babysitting my nieces Ariel and Marie Lee is a lot different from having my own child that I have to deal with day in and day out. That's a completely different ballgame."

Bryce nodded. "Ain't that the truth. Marie Lee is a handful, that's for sure. God bless Willow, she's definitely the mom to Marie Lee my ex never could be."

Bart continued to poke me with a stick, but I wouldn't jump to his game. I knew I needed to go over and at least talk to Sadie, but I'd do it on my own watch when I knew the time was right. Sadie was a delicate creature, and if caught too much off-guard, she'd retreat into her shell. I didn't want that to happen, especially since I had plans for us tonight.

If she wanted to partake in them.

I mean, ever since we'd been running into each other more, our conversations had been stiff. But, still familiar, and that was the refreshing part. Sadie had always been a breath of fresh air, but she also reminded me of a time in my life where I was the happiest I'd ever been. I got to relive a bit of that happiness whenever we talked. Even if the conversation was stilted and one-sided.

Despite the heartache that I knew I caused her, Sadie's

presence still felt like home. It always had. And I wasn't ready to lose that feeling.

So, I walked up to her. "Hey there, Sadie."

She stopped laughing and turned around. "Oh. Hey there, Will."

I nodded down at her glass. "Would you like another drink? I'm about to refill my whiskey."

"Actually? I think I'm going to nurse this for a bit until I can eat some food. Third glass and all."

My eyebrows rose. "I've never known you to have more than two."

She shrugged, her eyes locked with mine. "Well, things change over time."

I grinned. "I suppose they do."

She drew in a deep breath. "So!"

"So."

"What have you been up to lately?"

I shrugged. "Oh, you know. Just the rodeo and working at the family business."

"How are your parents doing, by the way? They went to Italy, right?"

I nodded. "Yes, they did. Naples, to be exact. And they are loving every second of it. We're all supposed to fly out to see them this Christmas and stay through New Year's."

"Oh, that's so exciting! Are you going to take lots of pictures?"

"Depends. Would you care to see them after I do?"

She smiled. "You know I've always wanted to travel. I'd love to see pictures."

"Then, I'll take as many as you want."

When she smiled up at me, my entire world came to a screeching halt. After all these years, she still had that effect on me, and it robbed me of my very breath. Even in just that short amount of time, we went from stilted conversation to easily bantering back and forth, like we'd always done. And the familiarity I felt whenever I was around her came rushing back, along with all the memories.

"Food's ready!" Bryce called out.

"Come and get it!" Bart yelled.

Sadie pointed. "Guess that's our cue."

I plucked her wine glass from her hand. "Then, allow me to freshen this up for you. I'll be right back."

The cookout was splendid. The food was phenomenal, as always. Bryce was a master griller, and Bart had a way around casseroles and vegetables that could spin anyone's head on their shoulders. And with all of the food came fluid conversation and laughter. Jokes and stories. Catching up and learning new things, including the fact that Sadie was a lightweight.

And after my third glass of whiskey, I felt bold.

I leaned down into Sadie's ear as she sat beside me. "You got any plans for your evening?"

Those doe eyes of hers slowly looked up at me. "Why?"

I grinned. "Got a cabin by a small pond with our name on it, if you'd like to come see my place. It's just through those woods, right here on the property."

She quirked an eyebrow. "Is this what do you with all of your women?"

I paused. "I'm not following."

She threw back the last of her wine. "I've heard the rumors about you and other women, Will. How all of your dates end in this way. You and them, going back to your place. Showing them around. Showing them to your bedroom..."

"Well, this isn't a date, is it?"

Something flashed behind her eyes, but it dwindled so quickly that I couldn't place it. I knew enough about her expressions, though, to know that the twitch in the left corner of her lip meant I had hurt her with my words.

"I'm sorry. I didn't mean t--."

She popped her lips. "The invitation is kind, but I'm afraid--."

I took her hand before she could finish her rejection. "Whatever line you draw for tonight, you have my word that I'll keep. I just want to spend more time with you, Sadie. However that time is spent, is solely up to you. Okay?"

Her eyes dropped to our connection. "Promise?"

I tucked some hair behind her ear with my free hand. "I promise with everything inside of me."

Then, her eyes looked back up at me, and I knew I had her. For once, the universe decided to play in my favor, and I wasn't about to ruin the opportunity.

"I suppose getting away from the crowd for a bit would be nice," she said.

I offered her my arm. "Then, allow me."

And the smile that crossed her cheeks lit up my entire world, causing me to make a solemn vow as we both stood from the picnic table.

I'll do whatever it takes to prove to her I'm the man she always knew me to be.

I just needed her to give me enough time to show her.

7

Sadie

As I gazed out the living room window of Will's incredible cabin in the middle of the woods, my eyes scanned over the expanse of the front yard. An acre and a half in front of me impeccably mowed and tailored to its surroundings. Wildflowers were still in bloom despite the first cold snap that was ushering fall into town, and the pond off in the distance glistened beneath the rising moonlight. I felt his presence behind me as I sipped my glass of water, trying to drown out the tipsiness I felt rattling around inside of my head.

Then, I felt his warmth at my side as we shared the window. Both of us, gazing outside.

"Looks like it might storm with those clouds," Will said.

I nodded slowly. "They'll be packing up the cookout fairly soon, I'm sure."

Thunder rumbled off in the distance. "Guess we left just in time, then."

I sipped my water again. "I guess we did."

I had a question running around in my head, so I decided to spit it out.

I drew in a deep breath through my nose. "What are we doing, Will?"

I turned my gaze up to his and found him already looking down at me. Which was a bit unnerving, but also curious.

"What?" I asked.

He blinked rapidly. "I'm sorry, what was your question?"

I furrowed my brow. "You okay?"

He cleared his throat. "Yeah. Yeah, I'm good. Just shocked, is all."

"Shocked? At what?"

He chuckled. "At the fact that you're in my home, for starters."

I turned to face him. "How long have you been living out here, anyway?"

"Essentially since I graduated from college. I was paying rent to my parents up until that point until Dad retired and handed the company over to us. With my first real paycheck, I bought this place outright. Including the five acres of space around it."

"But, we're still on the ranch, technically. Right?"

He nodded. "Yep. Bryce owns the other twenty or so

acres. But, these five right here in the middle, I own myself...
and, of course, Dad and Mom own the rest."

"Well, good for you."

He grinned. "Yes. Good for me, I suppose."

I cocked my head. "You suppose?"

He shrugged. "I don't know. I love the quiet, and I've got a
great garden going out back. But, it does get a bit too quiet
sometimes. A bit too lonely."

My eyes widened. "You have a garden?"

He blinked. "Well, yeah. Out back."

"A garden of your own."

"That's what I said."

"That you keep up?"

He snickered. "Seems like I'm not the only one of us that's
shocked."

I shook my head. "The last time I tried to get you to do
anything outside, you gave me this long spiel--."

He nodded in agreement. "I remember that argument.
You wanted to take a hike and go swimming in the lake, and I
said--."

I matched his voice as we spoke in unison. "—'there are
plenty of things we can do to exercise that have nothing to do
with anything outside.'"

My giggles rose, and a chuckle bubbled up the back of his
throat. Damn it, being here with him felt natural. Normal. As
if this was how it always should've been. And the more I tried
shaking that feeling, the more it held me hostage. Like one of
those knots you try to untie, but the knot itself only gets

tighter with more exertion. I felt trapped, but I didn't feel panicked. I felt cornered, but I didn't feel threatened.

It was an odd feeling.

And one I didn't want to let go.

"Well, that argument happened years ago, Sadie. I'm a much different person now. I'm not some reckless college kid any longer. I'm a man," Will said.

I felt heat trickle down the nape of my neck. "Yes. I suppose you are."

He grinned. "Suppose?"

I shrugged. "I'll give you the benefit of the doubt, sure."

"What? You don't agree?"

"I haven't been around you long enough to know whether I agree or disagree."

His arm threaded around my waist. "Well, in that case, why don't I pull you a bit closer so you can feel for yourself?"

My eyes fluttered closed as he drew me against him, and he wasn't wrong. He had muscles chiseled against his body that he'd never had back in high school. I couldn't help but inhale his woodland scent. The smell of oak and rustic wood filled the air as a hint of honey brought a sweetness to his scent that made my mouth water. I forced my eyes to open and gazed up into his, feeling my water glass being plucked from my hand.

Then, he wrapped me up in both of his arms and held me close against his body.

It felt so good to have him against me again. The feeling of home and safety rushed over me, leaving me breathless. I nuzzled my head against his chest, placing my ear against his heartbeat. And as I lulled myself back to calmness with the rhythmic thumping of his heart, I smiled.

I genuinely smiled as Will held me close to him.

Be careful, Sadie. So many other women have been here before you.

When the thought crossed my mind, I expected shame to take hold: shame, or embarrassment, or even more weakness. I didn't feel any of those things, though. Sure, I felt confused. It was hard to sort through everything with alcohol still rushing through my veins. But, I felt in control of my faculties. Of my thoughts. Of my movements and my wishes.

And with all my heart, I wished for Will to kiss me.

How can something so wrong feel so right?

"Sadie."

I slowly looked up into his face. "Yeah?"

His eyes met mine. "You look beautiful tonight."

I smiled softly. "You really think so?"

He tucked a strand of hair behind my ear. "I know so. I'm staring at you right now."

My smile overtook my face as he crooked his finger beneath my chin. And at that moment, I made a decision. I decided to cave to him instead of fight. I decided to give him my all instead of withholding it any longer. I didn't care what Will had done to me in the past. I didn't care about the heartache; I still felt throbbing deep within my soul. I didn't care about any of it.

All I cared about was feeling closer to the only person who really felt like home to me.

"Will," I whispered.

He paused just beyond my lips. "Tell me 'no,' and I'll stop."

I couldn't, though. I couldn't tell the love of my life to stop, even if I wanted to. I was helpless toward his advances. I had been enslaved by those glittering eyes and trapped against his pulsing muscles that coated his arms. And I wasn't even sorry about it.

So, I took it upon myself to close the gap between us.

The second our lips connected, my entire world shifted into place. Will's tongue pierced my lips, sliding effortlessly across the roof of my mouth. I felt on top of the world as he picked me up, sitting me down on the deep-set windowsill we had just been gazing out of together. His hands planted against the window. He pinned me against the cool surface with his body. And as my hands flew into his hair, pulling him even closer to me, I felt my body caving to him.

I felt my heart caving to him.

And I adored every second of it.

8

Will

I growled as I pressed her against the window. I trembled as my hands worked along her curves her body had blossomed over the years. Long gone was the lanky, boney body of her high school days, and in its place had grown a woman with enough softness to cradle my entire body. I wanted all of her against me. Every inch of her spread out for me like a buffet to enjoy for the rest of my night.

The rest of my days, really.

The way her tongue slid against my own—the way her hands raked through my hair. I felt passion wafting through her the way it rushed through my veins. Her legs parted for me, dripping a warmth against my clothed cock that made my breath hitch in my throat.

And as my forehead pressed against hers, I gazed deeply into her eyes.

"Sadie?" I asked.

She panted softly. "Hmm?"

"You're delightful, you know that?"

She smiled. "Kiss me again, you idiot."

I chuckled as my lips connected with hers, and I wrapped my arms around her. I wanted her against me, grinding around my dick. But, I didn't want anyone else seeing her in such a vulnerable state. Sadie was mine. Always had been, always would be. And I damn sure wasn't going to put her in that kind of situation.

Especially since she had always been so private.

With my hands cradling her ass cheeks, I walked her back into my bedroom. Our bodies collapsed to the mattress, my dick leaking with a need for her. I pinned her hands above her head and suckled on her lower lip. And the more she bucked against me, the weaker I became to her advances.

"Fucking hell," I grumbled.

"Take me. You can have me, Will," she gasped.

I paused. "What?"

Her half-hooded eyes met my own. "Huh?"

I cocked my head as I hovered above her. "Sadie, you have to be kidding."

Her face paled. "What? What did I do?"

I slowly sat up. "You're still a virgin?"

She swallowed hard. "I just ruined things, didn't I?"

I sighed. "No. You didn't ruin them. I just--that's a big thing, you know?"

She propped herself up. "I know. Which is why I haven't given it away yet."

"But... you just told me to take it."

Her eyes danced between mine. "Yes."

I held her gaze. "Are you sure?"

She moved around until she was planted on her knees on my mattress. And one by one, she shed her clothes. Off came her shirt, allowing me a wonderful glimpse of her glorious breasts before her bra came off. Then, she stood to her feet, teetering toward me as my hands gripped her hips to make sure she didn't fall. And as she wiggled out of the rest of her clothes--tossing them over the edge of the bed--her womanhood was right there. Her lower lips, glistening with want for me.

The smell of her. The taste of her. Having her again, just like this.

It was too much to bear for one man.

Before she could say another word, I dove in deep. Her hands fisted my hair, pulling me closer as I devoured that sweet little pussy of hers. My tongue pierced her folds, finding that sensitive nub I had learned to work with pride. My tongue swirled. My lips suckled. And I felt her quivering against the whole of me.

Then, I felt it.

I felt her entire body tightening up.

"Will, I can't. I have to--it's so--Will! Please!"

"Come for me," I growled.

And my words were all it took.

"Will! Yes! Holy shit!"

Her juices dripped down the slope of my neck as she collapsed against my shoulder. Her hands slid from my hair, trying to find something around her to latch onto as I caught her in my arms. She quaked against my grip as I laid her against the mattress, splaying her hair out along my crimson red pillows.

"You've never looked so beautiful," I whispered.

"What?" she asked groggily.

I stuffed the sentiment down. "Ready to become a woman, Sadie?"

She snickered. "Just let me have you already. Please."

She parted her legs for me, and my head started spinning off its axis. I felt the tip of my cock catch at her tight little entrance, and I steeled myself against the pleasure I knew I'd never experience again in all my life. As I looked down into Sadie's eyes, pinning her hands over her head once more, I felt my heart stop in my chest.

And as my cock pushed inside of her--inch by inch--I watched pleasure wash over her face.

"Oh, holy fuck," she groaned.

She felt like heaven. "Shit, Sadie."

"Will, don't stop. Keep--just keep--oh."

I growled. "So fucking tight. Good God in heaven."

My face fell to the crook of her neck as my hips bottomed out against hers. And as I felt her juices dripping down my balls, it urged me to move. Slowly, and deftly, I rocked against her. Feeling her walls caving to me as her body opened itself up for the first time. I'd never felt anything like it. I'd never had Sadie in any way like this before. And with every thrust against her softness--every thrust that brought me closer to ecstasy--I caved to her presence.

I knew this wouldn't be the last time I'd want her.

And I had to make sure she stayed at my side.

"Fucking hell," I hissed.

"Faster. Go faster. I'm so close, Will. I can't--it's so--you're--Will!"

The sounds of skin slapping skin filled the room. Her juices sprayed against my thighs as she let loose, with sounds spilling from her lips that I'd never heard before. Her dirty mouth only spurred me on, her tits jiggling against me as I pounded against her body.

Then, with stuttering hips and quivering walls, we caved together.

And her orgasm pulled mine from my body.

"Will! Shit! I'm co--mi--ng."

I collapsed against her, my cock still buried inside her pussy. "Oh fuck, Sadie. What the hell?"

Thread after thread of arousal shot from my tip, coating her virgin walls as they pulsed. Pulling from my balls every ounce of come I had for her. I panted against her shoulder. I kissed her delicate skin as her hands ran up and down the expanse of my back.

But, before I could whisper just how much she still meant

to me, her voice filled my ear with something that turned my stomach.

Something that would throw a wrench in my plans.

"You know this is only a one-time thing, right?" she asked softly.

I felt my heart breaking. But, it wasn't as if it came as a shock. I was the man who had broken her heart first. It was only fair she got to break mine in return.

So, instead of fighting, I simply kissed her shoulder. "I know."

Silence hung between us for a while before she finally eased me off.

"I should start getting dressed," she whispered.

I wanted to stop her. As I stared up at the ceiling, listening to her pad around and gathering up her clothes, I wanted to reach out for her. I wanted to gaze into those gorgeous eyes of hers and tell her how sorry I was for what happened between us. That I'd been punishing myself for losing her every single fucking day since she'd ended things with me. My brain screamed at me to start talking. My legs begged me to get up and stand in front of the doorway leading out of my bedroom.

But, I decided to give into her for once. I decided not to force her to mold to me like I had tried in the past. Because my decisions in the past had only gotten me to this point, and I didn't like this point.

Which meant I needed to try something different.

"Here," I grunted as I sat up, "let me give you a ride or

something."

She walked out of the room. "I can just call Willow or Luna. They can come get me."

I slid off the bed and reached for my clothes. "Please, Sadie. It's the least I can do!"

Her voice wafted down the hallway. "I promise I've got it. Don't worry about it!"

I rushed around to get my clothes back on, but once I got back out into the kitchen, I saw her holding up her phone.

"Willow's on her way," she said softly.

I tried not to show the pain I was feeling inside. "Well, at least I know you'll be safe."

She sighed. "I really did have a nice time with you today. Thank you."

I grinned. "I always have a nice time with you, Sadiebee. No need to thank me for anything."

She swallowed hard. "I'll go wait for her outside."

I walked toward her. "Why don't we sit and talk until she gets here? I'm pretty sure it was raining while we were--."

She ripped my front door open. "It's not raining. It'll be fine. Thanks for everything, Will."

I resisted the urge to run out after her and instead watched her stand outside while she waited for Willow. I knew it wouldn't take her any time at all to get here, so I took in as much of Sadie as I could. I studied her outfit, committing this entire night to memory. I tried to hang onto the scent of her body and the sounds she made just a few minutes ago as my body blanketed hers away from the world. But, as I stood there watching with lightning flashing in the distance, it lit up enough of the world to watch Sadie wipe at her eyes.

And finally, reality hit me.

You made her cry, you asshole. You're definitely not the man for her.

Lights came from my backyard, and I knew Willow was here. And as I watched Sadie continuing to wipe at her eyes, the rest of what was left of my heart shattered into a million pieces. If it was that easy for me to make this beautiful woman cry, then maybe our time really had passed. Maybe I had my chance and completely squandered it.

The least Sadie deserved was a man to make her smile. Not cry.

But, as I watched her climb into Willow's SUV, I felt something tugging at my soul. I felt extreme loneliness as I watched Sadie drive away. It greatly contrasted the wonderful feeling I had whenever she was in my arms. At my side. In my home.

And maybe--just maybe--it was the only feeling I needed to fix things. To give me the shove to take a leap of faith so we could finally be together they way my soul knew we were meant to be.

I just had to stop being a fucking coward long enough to see shit through.

ꕥ 9 ꕥ

Sadie

"Halt."

I settled my voice and let the command roll off the tip of my tongue. And to my amazement, Curly actually listened. I had purchased my latest riding sheep from an animal rescue shelter and rehabilitated her back to health. But, now that Curly was strong and well, I wanted to see if I could add Curly to my exhibit somehow.

The sheep-riding was hands down, my most requested attraction. Parents loved taking pictures of their children on top of the fluffy animals, and most of the kids enjoyed petting them and brushing them and feeding them out of little buckets they carried around. But, Curly had been a stubborn one.

More stubborn than the actual mule I had trained for my business as well.

But, even with the victory, I felt lackluster when it came to celebrating it. Curly walked up to me and gladly took the treats from my hands. However, I had to force myself to get down on my knees and hug and praise her. Usually, I made a big spectacle out of it. You know, to let the animals know that I was genuinely happy with what they were doing.

It took a lot of effort this time around, though.

And all because of him.

Will had taken up space in my mind that I couldn't afford to have taken. But, ever since our encounter a week ago, I couldn't get him off my mind. Every time I fell asleep, there he was. Kissing me and caressing me. Whispering how beautiful I was into my ear as my body writhed beneath his. And no matter how hard I tried--no matter what I took to help me sleep deeply--I still woke up with his naked body plastered across my mind.

I stood and clapped my hands. "Lunchtime, everyone! Come and get it!"

I walked over to a bell by the front doors of the barn and started ringing. And when I did, everyone came running. My sheep and my fainting goats. My miniature horses and my beautiful mule, Lioness.

Then, I set my sights on getting everyone fed.

And even then, Will still haunted me.

"Yes, ma'am. Down here is where the barn is. It's downslope from the house, but if you set up a nice water purification system, you can actually utilize all of that rainwater for your own uses for your animals."

I paused at the sound of my landlord's voice. "Randolph?"

His voice paused. "Sadie? Are you back here?"

I smiled as I petted Lioness while she ate. "I am! It's training day for me. Everything all right?"

But, when I saw him poke his head around the corner with a couple in tow, I knew this wasn't good news.

"Randolph?" I asked.

My landlord walked up to me with a plastered-on smile. "Sadie. I want you to meet Mr. and Mrs. Beauregard."

I wiped my hands off. "It's nice to meet you. Don't worry, just been feeding my menagerie."

The man shook my hand. "No worries. We've got animals ourselves."

"Oh, really?! What kind?"

The woman shook my hand, as well. "A couple of horses. Our two dogs. And how many chickens do we have now?"

The man smiled. "Fourteen, honey."

I giggled. "Gotta love those fresh eggs."

The woman giggled. "And the fresh chicken. Though, I can't stand to pluck the feathers. Lyle over here has to do that part."

The man shrugged. "Not really a big deal. I grew up living off the land, so it doesn't turn my stomach like it does my wife's."

I nodded. "Right, right. So, what can I help you guys with?"

My landlord sighed. "Actually, I need to give them a tour of the ground."

I blinked. "Why's that?"

Randolph's smile faltered. "They're here to see the property. They are interested in buying it."

A shockwave of silence rolled through my body as my mind turned over every single way it could go wrong. I imagined myself, out on the streets, having to sell off my animals. Not being able to find a new place for all of us. I tried my best not to let the shock register on my face, but I felt the couple staring at me with pitiful glances.

Randolph approached me. "Sadie, I'm so sorry. It's not a done deal yet, but we can talk later. Yeah? We just need the barn for a bit."

I looked up at him. "Don't you need to provide notice before doing something like this?"

His voice lowered to a whisper. "This was last-minute, I swear. I'm not even advertising. They drove by, liked what they saw, so they looked me up. That's it."

"Uh-huh."

"I'm just showing them around. Nothing is set in stone, but..."

I furrowed my brow. "But what?"

He sighed. "Look, I've had ideas of selling for a couple of years now. And I'd give you the benefit of the doubt if you wanted to buy this place yourself. But, I just can't keep it up anymore. Martha's going through a second round of chemo, and we could really use--."

I placed my hand on his shoulder. "When in the world was Martha diagnosed again? I thought she was in remission?"

Randolph's eyes watered over. "Just let me show them the barn, then we can talk. Okay? Shouldn't take more than half an hour."

I nodded. "Of course. Let me just get my crew some water and finish off their lunch, then I'll get out of your hair."

After bidding goodbye to the couple and staying in the shadows with my animals, I tried to overhear as much of what they were talking about as possible. But, that was hard with Randolph moving in the opposite directions of where I perched. So, I braced myself for the inevitable and made my way back to the house.

But that didn't stop me from watching them from the kitchen windows.

I mean, I always knew this could happen, especially since I'd been renting from Randolph month to month for the past two years. But, I figured I would have been given at least some sort of notice. Even if it was last-minute like this.

"I don't know what I'm gonna do," I whispered to myself.

All I can do is what I can do.

Will's words from high school echoed off the corners of my mind as I made my way for my bedroom. And as I eyed my laptop, I resigned myself to pushing off the rest of my day of training in favor of looking up other places to rent. A long time ago, back when I didn't know how to cope with my anxiety, Will would always chant that phrase softly in my ear whenever I got too worked up. He'd wrap me up in his arms, pepper my forehead with kisses, and constantly whisper that short phrase for only my ears to hear.

All you can do is what you can do, Sadiebee.

"All I can do is what I can do," I murmured to myself.

My fingers started flying across the keyboard as I started doing research. I pulled up all of the rental property websites I could search on Google and started entering my parameters. I needed at least two acres of land with a barn. The condition of the main house didn't concern me. But, I was concerned about finding enough space for my animals wherever I ended up.

And that task proved to be more difficult than I figured it might be.

All of the things I bookmarked were either out of my price range or not centrally located to where I needed to be, which meant more fuel costs to get to rodeo events. Even only an hour into searching for possible new places, I found myself already growing defeated.

"Come on," I grumbled.

In the middle of my typing, I heard the back door open, and my laptop went flying to the mattress. I shot up to my feet and held my breath as I heard footsteps padding through the kitchen, heading for the small hallway that led straight to the front of the house. I cracked my door open to try and hear what they were saying. But, all I caught were stupid words that didn't help me pinpoint anything.

And as I slipped out of my room, I heard the front door close before my landlord said my name.

"Sadie."

I jumped at the sound of his voice. "Holy shit! I mean, shoot. I mean, uh, sorry."

He chuckled. "It's okay. I don't blame you one bit."

I wrung my hands in front of me. "So? What's the verdict?"

He leaned against the front door. "I was planning on selling the house, but I wasn't going to put it up until after the winter. Figured the house wouldn't get many hits until then."

I pointed at the door. "Until they happened."

He shook his head. "Sadie, they're willing to give me two hundred grand for this place. No inspection necessary."

I nodded slowly. "Sounds like a fantastic deal."

"Yeah, and it could help out a lot with Martha's medical debt."

I sighed. "I thought she was doing okay, Randolph. What happened?"

He shrugged. "Your guess is as good as mine. One day, she's all right. And the next, she's face down on the bathroom floor because she passed out."

"I'm so sorry."

"Sadie, if you can somehow swing the original price I would've put on this house, it's yours. I know you love this place."

"I mean, I'm not really in a position to purchase anything right now. I don't even have a down payment."

"I'd work with you on that. I'd even take out the mortgage

myself and just let you keep paying me. Like a rent to own situation."

I chewed on my lower lip. "How much?"

He cleared his throat. "One fifty."

I crunched numbers quickly in my head, but it didn't do much.

"I can't afford that kind of a monthly payment for any sort of dwelling space. Six hundred is pushing it some months for me, and that kind of price for a home would easily push me into the eight hundreds. Especially with no down payment."

"You sure you don't want to take some time to sit on things and run accurate numbers?"

I closed my eyes. "Yeah, yeah. I'll sit down with someone who can run it for me down to the penny. But, I still don't think it's something I can swing."

"Well, as much as I hate to do it because you are like family, I have to do what's right by my wife. And if there's an offer on this place that could really help us out, I can't turn it down."

I drew in a sobering breath. "I understand, I promise. Just--let me find someone to help me with the numbers, and I'll get back to you. Say, the beginning of next week?"

He reached for the doorknob. "That's fine with me. But, this is your official notice: if you can't buy the place, I'm going to let that couple purchase it. I can negotiate a sixty-day closing instead of a thirty-day to give you some time to figure things out--."

I waved my hand in the air. "It's okay. I promise. I'll talk to you soon, all right? You just go be with your wife."

His eyes met mine. "I really am sorry, Sadie."

I nodded. "I know. And I promise you, it's okay. It's going to be okay, and Martha is going to pull through this. Just like she already has."

He gave me a grateful nod and walked out the front door. But, when he closed it behind him, I collapsed to the floor. I put my face in my hands and let the tears flow as all of the weight piling on top of my shoulders finally sank me to the ground.

"All I can do i-i-i-is--is what I can--can do."

Even as I chanted that phrase to myself, though, I felt more helpless than ever before. I felt more abandoned than I'd ever had in my entire life.

And in two months, if I couldn't find somewhere else to live, I'd be homeless.

10

Will

"Please, Willow? I'll owe you a massive favor."

She sighed. "Will, come on. If you don't have her number and address now, then she doesn't want you to have it."

"Look, I'm telling you: things went great between us the other night. I just want to send her some flowers. That's it."

"Then, send me the money, and I'll send them on your behalf."

I snickered. "You really think I'm going to do that?"

"Do you really think I'm going to give out my best friend's information to her ex?"

I leaned against the wall. "You're the one that invited everyone to this surprise cookout of yours... that we've never done before, might I add. You really mean to tell me you weren't secretly orchestrating getting us in the same room together?"

She cleared her throat. "Well, whatever the case might have been, if you don't have that information, then she doesn't want you to have it."

"I'll send you some flowers, too."

"Bribery gets you nowhere with me."

I grinned. "What if I babysit for a weekend?"

She paused. "Come again?"

"Yeah! I'll be happy to do it. You and Bryce plan a nice little getaway and let the kids come stay with me. I'll have them gardening and napping and watching movies and cooking food with me. You know, the works."

"All weekend?"

"Even a long weekend, if you'd like. Friday, Saturday, and Sunday. You can get the kids Monday morning. My treat."

"Uh-huh. And how much does this cost me?"

I smiled brightly. "Not a single fucking thing."

She groaned. "I hate you, you know that?"

I chuckled. "You can text her information to me. And if she asks? I'll let her know that my sleuthing skills online are top-notch."

"All right, all right. I'm sending it to you now. But when I plan this weekend? Don't start making excuses. Otherwise, I'll tell Sadie exactly how you manipulated me."

I barked with laughter. "Love you, too."

"Okay. Got it sent off. You got it on your end?"

75

I felt my phone vibrate against my cheek. "Got it."

"I'll contact you soon with the details!"

I pushed off from the wall. "Looking forward to it. Give the kids kisses for me."

"You can do that yourself next month when you take them for a long weekend."

My eyebrows rose. "Already planning?"

She giggled. "Just sent a text to Bryce to tell him to secure the dates on his work schedule."

"I really appreciate this, Willow."

"Don't thank me yet. She might kill us both for it."

"Nah. Sadie's always been a pacifist in that way. Really evens me out."

Her voice grew stern. "And if you fuck this up--if you hurt her again--."

I shook my head. "I won't, Willow. You have my word."

She sighed heavily. "Okay. Let me know how things go."

"Will do. Love you."

"Love you, too."

I hung up the phone with her and immediately started ordering a massive bouquet of summer flowers just for Sadie. And a pair of new boots, too. Those things caught my eye at the rodeo a couple of weeks back, and not in a good way. They were raggedy and worn. Old as hell, even to an untrained eye. I wanted her to have a decent pair of work boots if she was going to be a professional woman at a professional rodeo with her own damn business.

As good of a start as any to win her back.

After solidifying the orders, I started getting ready for my day. I knew I had to catch Willow early in the morning in order to have a shot at getting her to agree to my plan. And now, my five-in-the-morning alarm had paid off. I relegated myself to a long, hot shower and dressed in one of my more decadent suits. I was feeling powerful and on top of the world. I wanted to showcase it to everyone who wanted to have a glance at me.

Then, I made my way into work.

"Morning, Mr. Remington."

"Looking sharp, Mr. Remington."

"Is that a new suit, Mr. Remington?"

I smiled and waved at everyone who bombarded me with questions as I walked through the front doors. Our petroleum company had grown exponentially ever since Mom and Dad turned it over to us, and the small twenty-employee company had grown to over one hundred. And that was just at our headquarters in Houston. We kept it small here on the ranch. We had a dedicated office space attached to the horse training facility we had where we employed thirty individuals across a multitude of full-time and part-time positions. And almost every single one of them commented on something about my outfit. Or my smile. Or my countenance. Or the way I was walking.

Sadie looked good on me. She made me feel untouchable. Like I was the only man in the world equipped to solve everyone's problems.

Which meant I had to do everything in my power to get her at my side for good.

I went through the rigamarole of my day: paperwork, then conference calls, then training with Bryce. The day rushed by in the blink of an eye, and before I knew it, the clock had struck five. It was time to close up shop and wrap up training so we could all go home and get some damn good rest.

However, when I got back to my cabin, I decided to shoot Sadie a text.

Me: Did you like the flowers and the boots?

I figured a call might be too intrusive, but her number popped up on my screen attached to a phone call less than a minute after I sent that text. So, I picked up the phone. If the lovely lady wanted to hear my voice, that had to be a good sign.

Right?

"Well, hello there, beautiful," I said as I picked up the phone call.

"How did you get my information?" Sadie asked.

I blinked. "I work with computers and information most of my day. It doesn't take much to track things down."

"So, you're stalking me."

I furrowed my brow. "Not quite the reaction I was expecting, but we can take this route. No, I'm not stalking you. I just wanted to do something nice for you. That's all."

"By tracking down my information and sending me things I don't need."

I chuckled. "We both know that you need a new pair of

boots. I saw them at the rodeo. They're pretty worse for wear."

"They're my lucky boots. And besides, something doesn't have to look good to be functional. They've been broken in, and they're fine. I'm sending these boots back."

I sat at my kitchen table. "Can't. They're non-refundable. I hope you enjoy them."

"Everything is refundable nowadays, Will. Even with my business."

I blinked. "How can you return a petting zoo purchase?"

Her voice grew hardened. "That isn't the point. The point is, you got a grip on my information without my knowledge, and you sent me gifts because I guess that's how you operate. A few glasses of wine, a nice romp in the bed, and suddenly you're going to shower me with gifts like I'm your concubine. Well, I'm not, Will. I'm not your concubine, and I'm not a number for your little black book, and I'm certainly not--."

"Whoa, whoa, whoa, whoa. Okay. There's a massive misunderstanding here. Why don't we take it down a notch, breathe, and talk through this like adults? Yeah?"

Sadie drew in a deep breath. "I'm not a fan of text messaging."

I leaned back in my chair. "So I'm figuring out. That's good to know."

"I'm also not a fan of flowers. They die and make a mess that I eventually have to clean up."

"So, you're a chocolate person. Got it."

"Not much of a sweet tooth nowadays."

I snickered. "Since when? You had a massive one in high school."

She sighed. "Since I choked on a gummy bear during my senior year. I don't really go near sweets now. At least, not something I can easily choke on."

I nodded slowly. "Like small pieces of chocolate."

"Exactly."

I've missed so much of her life. "I'm sorry if you felt that I was intruding on your personal space. That wasn't my intention. I just wanted you to know that I had a great time with you last week, and I was thinking about you."

"And while it's appreciated, I don't need your gifts, Will. I don't need your money or your stuff, or whatever it is you do to keep yourself in the favor of women around here. I didn't need your stuff back in high school, and I don't need it now."

I grinned. "There are so many jokes to make, it's hard to hold back."

She paused. "Are you being serious right now."

I stood to my feet. "All right, all right. It was just a joke. Geez, you're wound tight today. Everything okay?"

"Look, we had a good time, right?"

"Riiiight...?"

"But that's all it was. One night of just experiencing something nice again. Something good and familiar."

A smile spread across my face. "It was nice, wasn't it."

She giggled. "Yes. It was. But that was it. That's where it ends with us."

"Even though we had a connection that I know you felt?"

"Like I said, that's where it ends."

"Even though I know how you feel and you know how I feel?"

She scoffed. "And how do you feel, Will?"

I licked my lips. "Like I have a lot of lost time to make up for after what I did."

"So, this is all about redemption for you."

"What? No."

"And what about all of the other women that I'm sure you have on your speed dial?"

I ran my hand through my hair. "Sadie, you're taking too much out of context. I'm just trying--."

"Yes, okay? I felt something with you. I felt like I did when I was back in high school. I felt safe and beautiful. I felt wanted and cherished."

"Because you *are*, Sadie. Don't you get it?"

She paused for a while before she sighed. "I can't do this. Especially not over the phone."

I saw my entrance and took it. "Then, come over. Let's talk face to face, maybe over some wine or--."

"No wine," she said quickly."

I grinned. "Water, then. Or some lemonade. I've got fresh lemonade in the refrigerator and snacks coming out of my ears. Come over, let's have lemonade and a snack, and we can talk about this face to face. Hash out everything."

"Everything?"

I nodded. "Going back as far as you want to go."

"Even all the way back to college?"

"Even all the way back to our middle school years, if that's what it takes."

She groaned. "Ugh, the braces."

"Hey, you forget I had those insane glasses for the longest time."

She howled with laughter. "Oh, my goodness! The white pair with the sparkles you didn't see in the store!"

I smiled so hard, my cheeks hurt. "Yeah. Wore those damn suckers for four years before Mom let me finally change them."

I listened to the sweet, beautiful sound of her laughter before it died down.

"Sadie?"

She cleared her throat. "Yes?"

"Just come over. Let's talk in person. And whatever happens, happens."

And to my shock, she agreed.

11

Sadie

The timber in the front doors swirled and spiraled before my very eyes as I stared at the entrance of Will's cabin. I had done it. I had gotten myself here. My truck's brakes groaned as I came to a stop. I heard metal tinkering around, adjusting to the cold snap that had fallen over our neck of the woods.

And yet, I couldn't bring myself to knock on the door.

What in the world was I doing there? I knew I didn't need to be there. What I needed to do was turn around, call the girls, and run for the hills.

"Call the girls. They'll tell you to run," I whispered to myself.

Well, maybe not Willow.

I still had no idea why in the world my best friend would give out my information like that. But, I couldn't say I completely hated her for it. She simply did what I didn't have the guts to do the last time I was over at Will's, so I really needed to be thanking her.

That didn't change the fact that I shouldn't have been caught up in my ex in the first place.

"You gonna keep standing out there? Or you gonna come inside?"

His voice pulled me from my trance, and my eyes quickly panned up his body. When in the world had the front door opened? How long had Will been staring at me?

I felt my muscles shiver as my eyes danced between his.

"Sorry. Just--in my head a bit," I said with a snicker.

He stepped off to the side. "Well, come on in, and we can be inside our heads together."

Oddly enough, relief washed through my veins. It helped to know that Will was just as nervous about this as I had apparently become. He ushered me back into his home, and my eyes gazed down the hallway toward his bedroom. It was there that my mind quickly ran away from me.

"I wasn't sure you were going to knock, to be honest," Will said.

I turned to face him. "I suppose I was debating that a bit myself."

He closed the door. "Wondering if you should call the girls?"

I smiled softly. "Some things never do change."

He shook his head. "You guys have always been close. It doesn't shock me one bit that the three of you are still friends to this day."

"I'm lucky to have them."

"And they're lucky to have you, Sadiebee."

Comfort, like the warm waves of a summer ocean, sloshed over my body at the sound of that nickname. He used to call me that all the time back when we were kids. Still together, still in love, and still hopeful about the world. His eyes met mine with that little sparkle I fell in love with the first time I ever laid eyes on him, and I felt my knees evaporate.

My legs, supported by nothing but jello.

But, I still needed to address things with him. "Will."

He slid his hands into his pockets. "Sadie."

I shook my head. "You can't buy my affections. You know that, right?"

"Is this the part where you say 'because I don't need your money' or 'because I don't need you'?"

I shrugged. "A bit of both?"

He puffed out his cheeks with a sigh. "Ouch."

"I mean, what did you expect, Will? One night of passion followed by some flowers, and suddenly, I forget everything that's happened?"

"You can't say you didn't feel something that night, Sadiebee."

I snickered. "Feeling something from an orgasm and feeling something from my heart are two very different things, *Willibee*."

He held up his hands in mock surrender. "All right, all right. The nickname is gone. All you had to do was ask."

My face fell flat. "Well, I asked you to love me and stay faithful to me when you went off to college, and we all see how that turned out."

"Damn it, I'm just trying to show you that I'm a changed man. That you're not just some other girl to me."

"Yeah, you've really changed from your fraternizing ways since college. I know your reputation around town. I've talked to more than my fair share of your conquests while out with the girls."

He took a step toward me. "So, you're saying people can't change? Are you saying that love doesn't change someone?"

"Are you saying you love me?"

"No! I mean, yes. I mean--Jesus, Sadie. Seriously?"

I folded my arms over my chest. "It's a simple 'yes' or 'no' question."

His eyes met mine. "Do you still love me?"

I licked my lips. "My point is: you weren't a billionaire when we were together in high school, so the fact that you feel the need to send me stuff like you did, is almost an insult. I don't care about your money, Will."

"I never thought you did. I just wanted to do something nice for you for once."

My arms fell to my sides. "Oh."

He shrugged. "You deserve nice things."

"Well, just because I deserve nice things doesn't mean I can have them."

He paused. "What does that mean?"

You're getting too emotional. Pull back. "Look, my point is--."

He took another step toward me. "No, no, no. No diverting. You always do that when something's wrong."

"This conversation isn't about me. It's about you."

"Well, I'm making it about you now. What did you mean by that statement? What do you need that you can't have, Sadie?"

I chewed on the inside of my lip. "Drop it. Or I'll leave."

He shook his head slowly. "Anyway... at the very least, you deserve a nice pair of boots to work in during rodeo season. That's the only place where my head was."

I quirked an eyebrow. "The *only* place?"

He rolled his eyes. "And I was hoping to see you again. But, you know, semantics."

I blinked. "You didn't send me those gifts to get me back in bed?"

He chuckled. "Is that what this town really thinks of me?"

And when I didn't answer, I could've sworn I saw hurt behind his eyes.

"I suppose I shouldn't be shocked. My dating life has been pretty much everywhere," he murmured.

I giggled. "Everywhere? Try everyone."

"All right, all right. Let's simmer down there a bit. I'm not that much of a manwhore."

I grinned. "Sure about that?"

He snickered before he started chuckling. "You always

were a spitfire whenever you were passionate about something."

"You really didn't send me those gifts just to get me back in bed?"

"I mean... I'm a man? I enjoyed what we shared. But then again, I always did. Always have."

Bite your tongue, he's opening up. "Have?"

"The truth?"

I nodded. "Yes. I want the truth."

He walked over to me until he was so close that I felt his body heat radiating against my chest.

"Sometimes, Sadie, I dated just to get rid of the thought of you. Because I knew there was no way in hell you'd ever take me back. That you'd ever consider giving me a second chance."

I tried to hang onto a shred of my strength. "Not very fair to the other girls."

He shook his head. "Maybe not. But, no matter who I was with and no matter what we did, every single time I wished it was you. So, when we ended up back here, and things happened I-I-I--I saw an opportunity? Thought maybe if I could capitalize on it, I might have a sliver of a chance to get back the one person who was ever in my life that I wish was still here."

Shock rooted me to the floor. "You're being serious right now."

His hands gripped my shoulders. "As serious as I'll ever get with you."

My heart warmed quickly in my chest as the wind kicked up outside. The chill of the impending fall and winter months that were steadily approaching only reminded me of my predicament, though. In a few more weeks, rodeo season would be over, and I no longer had a way of making money on the off-season. Not if I was going to be evicted in a couple of months. I felt weak against Will's grasp. I felt beautiful as he stared down at me with that cheeky little stare of his that always seemed to be smiling, even when he wasn't.

And the thing I needed the most was a distraction.

Even if it was only temporary.

"You know, coming over here and attempting to reason with the man that broke my heart all those years ago is definitely a... bad girl move."

Will's eyes twitched. "A what?"

I smiled sweetly up at him. "A bad girl move."

He swallowed hard. "I suppose it would be, yes."

I giggled. "And sometimes, a girl might enjoy being bad."

He grinned. "She does, does she?"

I took a small step away from him. "Maybe."

His eyes fell down my body. "And what if a man were to, say, be interested in this... bad girl."

I felt my breath hitch in my throat. "Do bad boys really ask, though?"

His growl was the next thing I heard before his hand wrapped around my neck. I gasped as he backed me against a wall, my hands splayed against the painted plaster. I felt his lips against the shell of my ear, his hot breath pulsing as my nipples began puckering against my bra.

"Does the bad girl want a piece of the big, bad wolf?" he asked.

And when my eyes fluttered closed, I knew I had found the distraction I needed.

"Yes," I whispered.

❦ 12 ❦

Will

I felt her trembling against my body, and it only served to stiffen my cock. 'Bad girl' was a term I used back when we had been dating to try and rile her up a bit, but I'd never known her to turn the tables and use it on me. Just hearing her say it was hot as fuck. Just feeling her puckered tits against my chest made me sizzling with desire. I stroked my thumb along her jawline as her eyes held my face, my leg pressed between her thighs.

And when I felt the warmth of her pussy, something inside me snapped.

"Come with me," I growled.

I hoisted her body against me and walked her over to the kitchen table. I wiped everything off with my hands, listening as it crashed to the floor. And with a giggle, I laid Sadie down on top of the table. I ripped at my clothes, casting my shirt aside and ripping my leather belt from the loops of my pants.

Then, I worked on getting Sadie out of her clothes.

My mouth fell everywhere that she allowed it. I wrapped my lips around her puckered nipples and curled my fingertips into her sweet excess. I nibbled and suckled against her skin, listening to her squeal and moan all in one breath.

And when we were clad in nothing but our skin, I hovered over her as the table held her weight.

"Do you know what happens to bad girls when they get caught?" I asked.

She walked her fingertips up my chest. "They get rewarded?"

I pinned her hands above her head. "No. They get punished."

In one swift movement, I lined my rock hard cock up to her entrance and barreled my way inside. Her eyes bulged as my hips snapped against hers, unwilling to give her a moment to breathe. Or even adjust. Her body bucked against my own as her sounds filled the space around us. The legs of my kitchen table scraped against the floor, accenting the sound of wet skin slapping against wet skin.

And when I felt her walls closing tightly around me, I gazed into her eyes.

"You're close, aren't you?" I grunted.

She gasped for air. "Will. You're so--I can't--oh, shit!"

I gnashed my teeth together. "That's it. Drench me in you. Come for me, Sadiebee. Be a good girl."

"Yes. Yes! I'm a good girl! Holy fuck!"

I hummed with pride as I bit into the meat of her breast, holding on tightly as she unraveled against my body. Her walls quivered around my cock as I released her hands, and she quickly attached them to my back. Her nails raked against my skin, filling me with pain that somehow only added to my pleasure.

I never wanted this moment to end.

"You're coming with me," I growled.

"Where are we--ah!"

I tossed Sadie over my shoulder and gave her pert little ass a nice swat. She yelped and giggled as she kicked her feet, taunting me with the smell of her sex. I stormed into my bedroom and dropped her onto the mattress. I gripped her hips and flipped her over before spanking her ass cheeks yet again. She raised them for me as she scooted to the edge of the bed, knowing exactly what I wanted.

"Such a good girl," I whispered.

I ran my hands over the red spots on her ass, and I heard her giggle against her arm. The sound made my heart grow two more sizes, filled with all the love in the world I had for this woman. I'd never stopped loving Sadie. No matter who I dated and no matter what I did, I never could get her out of my heart. She had made her home there, hellbent on torturing me until the day I died.

Yet, there she was with her ass in the air.

Waiting for my intrusion.

"Will," she breathed.

I gripped my cock. "I hope you're ready for a long night. Because you're not leaving until the morning."

I slammed myself back inside and listened to her beautiful wails of pleasure. Her back hollowed out as she fisted the sheets of my bed, her juices dripping down my balls. I gripped her hips and pulled her back into me. I fucked my cock with her body, listening as she moaned and choked out my name. It was a heady feeling, finally being able to have her like this. I had dreamt so much about it back in high school that I almost couldn't contain myself in her presence.

And now, all I wanted was to keep her with me forever.

"Shit, Sadie."

She gasped for air. "So close. So good. Holy fuck, fill me up, Will. Fill me up!"

"Because that's what good girls get, huh? A good cock? That what you want, you bad girl?"

"Yes."

"You want this cock?"

Her walls started tightening. "Keep going. I'm almost there. Keep going. Will. Keep going!"

A roar tore from my throat. "Fucking hell, Sadie!"

"William!"

I felt her collapse, and she took me with her. With my cock trapped against her tightening walls, I crashed against her back as my balls pulled up into my body. My body quaked with each spurt of arousal that shot from the tip of my dick, filling her as she shivered beneath me. Her moans echoed off the walls of my mind. The tightening of her entire body made my chest swell with pride, and my stomach filled with happiness. I'd never felt so fulfilled in all my life. Not with work. Not with love. Nothing.

It was Sadie who made all of this worthwhile.

"Will?" she murmured.

I slowly pulled out from between her legs. "Uh-huh?"

"Thirsty."

"Oh, oh, oh. Yes. Holy shit, hang on."

It took all of the remaining strength I had to press myself off her body, but I managed it.

"Need a hand?" I asked.

She didn't accept it. "I got it, but thank you."

I thumbed over my shoulder. "Let me go get you something to drink."

"Actually, I thought maybe we could get dressed and get some food? Or watch a movie or something?"

A slow smile crept across my face. "I'd love nothing more, Sadiebee."

She giggled. "I'm just going to go get my clothes."

"Or we could stay naked."

"Or, we could put on clothes and cuddle by the fire."

I wiggled my eyebrows. "And who's going to make that fire, huh?"

She pushed me playfully. "You're so crazy. Come on, I can get my own drink."

I gripped her arm. "How about this? You go get us a drink

to share, and I'll start a nice, warm shower for us. We can take one, see where it leads, and then we can dry off together and watch a movie all curled up in a blanket."

"Without clothes?"

I shrugged. "We can figure it out along the way."

She shook her head. "You're something else, you know that?"

I winked. "I try my best."

She walked over to the door. "Okay, I'll go get us a drink, and you start the shower. I'll be back in a couple of seconds."

"Sure thing, beautiful."

I watched her beautiful hips saunter and sway out of my bedroom before I booked it into the bathroom. I quickly flipped on the water and got the bathroom steaming up for us, then I raked my fingers through my hair. I smoothed my eyebrows down in the mirror and flexed my muscles, trying to make sure I looked my best for her viewing pleasure whenever she got back.

But, as the water continued to run, she didn't come back.

"Sadie?" I asked.

I reached for a towel and wrapped it around my own body before I went in search of her.

"Sadie! You all right!?"

I heard her sniffle. "I'm sorry, but I have to go, Will."

I rushed down the hallway. "Wait, wait, wait. What's happening?"

I saw her quickly wipe at her eyes. "I have an emergency. I'm so sorry. I have to go."

"Well, here. Let me throw some clothes on, and I can--."

"No, Will!"

In all the years I'd known--and loved--Sadie, I'd never heard her yell. I'd never heard her so much as raise her voice at someone, and yet the fervent and desperate nature of her voice echoed throughout my home. I furrowed my brow tightly as I watched her throw on the rest of her clothes. I clocked her reddened eyes and the wet tips of her fingers.

Sadie was crying.

And I was ready to wring the neck of whoever had hurt her.

"Sadie, talk to me," I said.

I walked over to her, but she practically jumped for the front door.

"I'll make it up to you. You can hold me to that," she said.

She went to open the door, but I closed it with my hand. "Look at me."

She tried opening the door again. "Will, let me go."

But, I kept closing it. "Not until you talk to me. What's wrong?"

"It's none of your concern anyway."

I gripped her shoulders and turned her to face me. "Despite what you may think in that head of yours, I'm not the same boy that I was back in college. I've grown up, Sadie. That was over a decade ago, what happened between us. And I've never stopped thinking about you. I've never *once* stopped loving you, whether you believe me or not."

Her lower lip started quivering. "I can't do this."

97

I brushed her tears away with my knuckles. "Do what?"

"This. I can't do this. I-i-i-it's--it's too much. And I just can't. I'm sorry."

She ripped the front door open and started rushing to her car, trying to get away from me as quickly as possible. I watched her pull her truck door open. I watched her practically throw herself down into her seat. She cranked that engine and sped down the gravel driveway, swerving she was trying to leave so quickly.

And the entire time I watched her, I had to fight the urge to throw her back over my shoulder. I had to fight the urge to chase after her because when Sadie had her mindset on something, nothing could derail her. So, if leaving was what she wanted, there was nothing I'd be able to do to stop her. It didn't stop me from worrying, though. It didn't stop me from wondering what in the hell had upset her so badly while she was out here. But, come hell or high water, I'd figure it out.

And I'd do whatever I could to fix it.

13

Sadie

I sniffled as I wiped the tears off my face. "I don't know what to do, you guys. I've got nowhere to go."

Willow shushed me softly. "Sh-sh-sh-sh-sh. Hey, it's gonna be okay."

Luna sighed. "When did your landlord tell you all of this?"

I scoffed. "Today. All of this stuff took place just today. He had them come out and view the property, we had a small discussion about him needing the money, and then I got a text about half an hour ago saying he accepted the offer on the house."

Willow cleared her throat. "You know you could always come stay with us until you find a place."

Luna piped up. "Hey! That's a good idea! They've got more than enough land for your animals, too."

I heard Willow's smile through the phone. "Yep. They'd be completely welcome here. You could stay in the guesthouse and help me out with the kids. We could have wine every single night."

I blinked. "Isn't that you and Bryce's thing, though?"

"I mean, it could be our thing for a few weeks."

I scoffed. "Unfortunately, I think it's going to take more than just a few weeks to find what I'm looking for. I mean, this place is perfect for me. The rent is affordable. It comes with the land I need, and the barn. Would you guys have a barn I could use?"

Willow paused. "Bryce could build one?"

Luna groaned. "This is such bullshit. Surely, there's a way you can stop this. Doesn't he legally have to give a warning or something like that?"

I nodded. "Yes, for move-out. But, nothing else. He's given me sixty days to find a place. Which is in accordance with local laws."

Luna hissed. "Damn it."

Willow sipped on a drink of some sort. "Well, the offer still stands. We can work something out if you're down to the wire and just need a place to stay. We'll even help you move. Just keep it in the back of your mind, all right?"

I flopped onto my bed, wiping at my tears. "I really appreciate it, thanks."

"You sure you don't want us to come over?" Luna asked.

"I could bring wine," Willow singsonged.

I pinched the bridge of my nose. "I'll figure something out. In the meantime, though, I need to clean this place up a bit. My landlord's going to have people in and out over the coming week to fix things that the buyers want fixed. Don't want to completely embarrass myself."

Willow giggled. "Let me guess. You left a pair of socks in the wrong drawer."

I paused. "What?"

Luna cackled with laughter. "Oh! I bet there's a small soap scum stain at the bottom of your tub."

Willow snickered. "You remember when she spilled that wine on her carpet and thought it was the end of the world?"

I rolled my eyes. "All right, I get it."

Luna giggled profusely. "My favorite is when she found all of that dust underneath the fridge when she moved it to have that new one installed. You remember that?"

Willow started howling. "She had to get down on her hands and knees right then and there and mop the floor. Those poor delivery guys were being held hostage by a woman with a mop!"

I clicked my tongue. "Right, well. Love you guys and thanks for the support!"

Luna scoffed. "Oh, come on. We were just--."

I hung up on my two best friends before they could get another word in edgewise at my expense. Was I a clean freak? Yes. Was I weirded out by germs? Most definitely.

Did I have to be teased about it? Absolutely not.

I had enough going on in my life already. I didn't need that shit, too.

"What am I gonna do?" I whispered to myself.

My phone started vibrating again in my hand, and I took a peek at it. The smallest part of me was hoping it might be Will. But, the upset part of me ignored a three-way phone call with the girls. I was over them, for the moment. However, my phone started vibrating again, and I knew they wouldn't stop until I picked it up.

Might as well make the conversation productive.

I answered the phone. "Willow?"

She sighed. "Girl, we shouldn't have teased you like that."

Luna piped up. "Yeah, it was selfish and mean. We should've known you wouldn't have been in a joking--."

I didn't care about their apologies. "Why did you give Will my information, Willow?"

Everyone on the phone fell silent as I sat up. And finally, Willow found the strength to answer.

"Your information?" she asked.

I stood to my feet. "I'm not stupid. I know you gave Will my contact information. I want to know why."

Luna sighed. "Did you really do that, Willow?"

I nodded slowly. "So, you were working alone. Now, I'm really curious as to the question."

Willow scoffed. "Oh, come on. You're not playing anyone for a fool, Sadie."

I furrowed my brow. "What?"

"I know damn good and well--as well as Luna--that you never once stopped loving Will."

I blinked. "So, that gives you the right to give out my information?"

"I don't believe Will's the same person he was back then. We were all just kids."

I balked. "He cheated on me and posted pictures of it on his own fucking social media outlets, all the while dodging my goddamn calls, Willow!"

Luna whistled softly. "Never good when she starts cussing."

I snarled. "You're damn right, it isn't. You had no right to do that, Willow. You have no right to give out my number or my address or anything of that matter. You don't have that kind of power in my life."

Willow sighed. "Would you just breathe for a second and get over yourself?"

Luna clicked her tongue. "Oh, boy."

My eyebrows rose. "What did you just say?"

Willow paused. "What I mean to say is that I believe you should give the man a second chance for everyone's sake. I know you care about him. And I happen to believe he cares about you, too."

I closed my eyes. "That still doesn't mean what you did was right."

"You're right. It wasn't. But, I'm not apologizing for it. I knew you wouldn't take that step on your own despite how we all see you looking at him whenever he crosses our path."

I felt fury rushing through my veins. "Let me get this straight: you're allowed to make all sorts of life decisions on my behalf without my input, and I'm supposed to thank you for it?"

Luna tried to settle us down. "Okay, okay, okay. I know everyone is wound pretty tight right now. But, why don't we--?"

Willow and I spoke in unison. "Shut up, Luna."

She murmured to herself. "Fine. Whatever."

I sucked air through my teeth. "You should have told me, at the very least. You should have told you gave out my information so I could have expected something. And you didn't even give me the courtesy of doing that."

Luna slurped on something on the other end of the line. "I'm with Sadie on this one."

"What!?" Willow exclaimed.

Luna snickered. "Sorry, girl. But, Sadie's right. If you were going to willy-nilly hand out her information--."

"It's not like I gave it to a stranger!"

Luna continued despite the interruption. "--then you should have told Sadie what you did. You shouldn't have kept it a secret."

I pointed into the air as if she were standing in front of me. "That's why I'm pissed. Yes, I'm upset you gave out my information. But, then, you didn't even have the courtesy to tell me what you'd done. It's like my personal information, as well as my feelings, didn't matter worth shit to you at that moment."

Willow sniffled. "You know damn good, and well, that isn't true."

I shook my head. "You're my friend. Not his. I don't care if you have a child with his brother. I don't care if you two live together. I don't care if you see him on a regular basis. You're supposed to be on my side. You're supposed to have my back. Not his. He made me believe there was a future for us when there was none. He made me believe I was the only girl for him, and he shattered my world. It took me months to get back on my feet."

Willow spoke softly. "I remember."

"Then, the next time you want to pull some shit like that with Will regarding me? Why don't you consider all of that next time?"

"I really think you're judging him too harshly, Sadie."

I snickered. "And if you really think this is all about judgment at this point, then you're blinder than I thought."

Luna drew in a short breath of air. "Actually, I do agree a bit with Willow?"

Willow and I spoke in unison this time. "What?"

Luna giggled. "I mean, the part about where Will's a totally different person. I believe that, too."

I propped my cell phone against my shoulder. "Well, he may be different on the inside, but his actions speak louder than whatever inner dialogue he's got going on. You guys know his reputation for women around town."

Willow sighed. "And why do you think that is, Sadie?"

I shrugged. "Why the hell do I care? He's still a womanizer and doesn't give a damn about their feelings. Obviously."

Luna hit me with a question that gave me pause. "And why do you think he hasn't settled down with any of them? I mean, at one point, he was dating a Hollywood B-list actress! Why in the world do you think the man hasn't attempted to settle down with someone since college?"

I snickered. "Well, I'll be the judge of that, Luna."

Willow started coughing on the other end of the line.

"Whoa, whoa, whoa. You okay over there?" I asked.

She kept coughing, and I started to grow worried.

"Willow. Breathe for us, girl," Luna said.

She choked out the words. "You'll... you'll judge?"

I paused. "Yeeeeeah?"

Luna gasped. "Wait a second. If you're going to be the judge of that, does that mean you're seeing Will?"

Uh oh. "I just meant--."

Willow's voice was hoarse. "Don't you even think about lying to us."

I scoffed. "That's rich, coming from you."

"Technically," Luna said before she slurped something again on the line, "she didn't lie. She just withheld information."

"Oh, so you're on her side now?"

Willow's voice grew in volume. "No, no, no, no. You don't get to corner us and us not corner you back. Does this mean you're seeing Will? Did me giving him your information actually work?"

"Gotta go, bye!"

"Wait, wait, wait, Sadie. N--!"

I hung up the phone before they could get another word in, yet again, and I pulled the battery out of my phone after the fact. The world felt as if it was spinning way too quickly, and my legs felt like jello, and my chest felt like it had the weight of the world settled against it. I felt sick to my stomach as I eased back down onto my bed, curling up into a ball on the edge of the mattress.

And as silent tears streaked my cheeks, only one thought rushed through my mind.

I wish Will were here to hold me even though I probably don't deserve it.

❧ 14 ❧

Will

Practical gifts? I can do practical gifts.

I propped my chin against my knuckles as I sat at the kitchen table. With my cell phone in my other hand, I scrolled through endless Google searches that came up after I typed in 'practical gifts for a girlfriend.' Granted, Sadie wasn't my girlfriend. But, I wanted her to be. And if I wanted her to be, I needed to start treating her like one.

Starting with finding the kinds of gifts she actually enjoyed.

The smell of my lukewarm coffee wafted up my nostrils as I scrolled through page sixteen of the Google search. Last night had turned up fruitless when it came to gifts I thought Sadie might enjoy, but I refused to give up. I knew I could nail this. I knew I could find the right gift for her to make her weak in her knees. I mean, every girl had a sweet spot. Every girl I'd ever been with had that one gift that made them collapse into my arms.

I needed to find that gift for Sadie.

It was my only shot at showing her how serious I was about this thing that had always been between us.

"Come on," I murmured.

I scrolled through a dozen or more pages while my coffee grew cold. But, once the crick in my neck popped up, I sat up straight at the kitchen table. I set my phone down and stretched my arms over my head, feeling my back pop into place numerous times.

"I need a new mattress," I groaned.

I abandoned my phone in order to freshen up my coffee while I kept racking my brain for presents. Sadie had never been a jewelry kind of girl, and even now, I never saw her wearing anything. A pair of earrings every now and again, sure. But, no rings or bracelets, or even ankle charms.

And she definitely wasn't a makeup person.

I grinned. "She doesn't need the shit, either."

I leaned against the kitchen counter and sipped my dark black coffee. I closed my eyes and let the burn trickle down my throat, pulling me out of the foggy haze the morning blanketed across my property. Waking up to a dimmed sun and fog across the grounds always felt equal parts relaxing and spooky. So, I snatched my phone up from the kitchen table and made my way out to the front porch.

Just so I could watch the fog undulate softly over my front lawn.

I knew Sadie didn't want me to try and buy her affections, but I enjoyed giving gifts. I enjoyed walking by a shop and being reminded of someone and having the capability to buy something for them just to see them smile. I had to figure out what made Sadie smile first. And while I had years of our childhood to draw from, that didn't mean those same principles still held.

I mean, I wasn't the same person I was as a teenager. So, I had to assume that neither was Sadie.

Passions don't change, though.

I had an entirely different train of thought to follow, so I swiped my phone open and started searching around again. Passions. Sadie's passion for animals hadn't changed one iota. If anything, it had only grown, and all I had to do was look at her business to tell that. And despite the fact that she chastised me for the boots, it wasn't as if she returned them to me.

Oh, no. She kept the gift.

And that got me wondering.

I started looking up all sorts of things she could use for her business. New, portable fencing that was easy to carry to and from a rodeo. A new fold-out table that also had attachments to turn it into a nice ticket booth.

"Or a cash register kiosk," I murmured to myself.

My thoughts pulled me back to that rodeo, and I tried to remember everything I could about that petting zoo she had out there. I tried to remember how many animals she had, but I hadn't been paying that much attention to it.

"Shit," I hissed.

I needed to pay more attention to things.

That one train of thought spiraled me down a hole, though. And a productive hole at that. I knew enough about where she lived to know that lawn care must've been a bitch. Especially for a single woman living by herself and running her own business. So, I started looking into lawn care services and how much they'd cost on a monthly basis. I even started looking at maid services, because if Sadie was still the neat-freak she'd always been, it might come as a relief to her to have someone else do the deep-cleaning for once.

"Oh, a landscaper. I could pay them extra to keep up a small garden."

I bookmarked things I found and slowly had a plan forming in my head. I wasn't sure if the slow morning had rebooted my mind or if the caffeine was finally beginning to kick in, but I felt on top of the world. I felt like I had finally nailed this, and I couldn't wait to surprise Sadie with these gifts along the way.

But, before I could request a quote from the landscaping company, a call from Bryce rolled through my phone.

So, I answered. "Morning, Biggie. To what do I owe the pleasure?"

He paused. "Did you just call me 'Biggie'?"

I grinned. "Yeah? And?"

"Right. Okay. Anyway, can I ask you something if you promise to be honest with me?"

"Uh... sure? Everything okay?"

He sighed. "What's going on with Sadie?"

"How the hell should I know?"

"Oh, cut the shit, Will. We all know Sadie left with you at the cookout the other day. And now, the girls are fighting over the phone at all hours of the morning, waking up the baby and shit. What gives? What did you do?"

I stood from my chair. "Why the fuck do you automatically assume I've done something wrong?"

"Because this is what you do, Will. You're infatuated for a bit, then you piss them off and run for the hills. What did you do?"

Anger bubbled my blood. "Sadie's different, and you know that. She's always been different."

"Then, please tell me the girls weren't fighting about you. Because I heard your name dropped several times last night. I won't have you dicking around with them."

My voice flattened. "Nice to know you've got my back."

"All I'm asking is whether or not you've done something. That's all."

I shrugged. "Haven't done shit except give her flowers and a new pair of work boots. That's all."

He paused. "That's all?"

I nodded. "Yep."

"What aren't you telling me?"

"I don't owe you every shred of my life, Bryce. I haven't

pissed Sadie off. If anything, she left my place the other day after a phone call that rattled her so badly she started crying."

"Wait, you had Sadie at your place? Since when?"

I rolled my eyes. "My point is that whatever happened on that phone call? That's what pissed her off."

"So, this wasn't you."

"Nope."

"Huh."

I furrowed my brow. "What do you know, Bryce?"

He cleared his throat. "It's just conjecture at this point."

I made my way inside. "If something's wrong with Sadie, I need to know."

"And why's that?"

"Because I love her, damn it. That's why!"

Everything around me came to a grinding halt as the words I just uttered hung heavily in the air. There they were as if I had just pulled them out of a hat, like a magic trick. I swallowed hard and closed my eyes, trying to contain the little bit of self-control I had left.

"I figured you still did, you know," Bryce finally said.

I flopped down at the kitchen table again. "Yeah, yeah."

"How long have you felt this way?"

"What makes you think I ever stopped?"

He sighed. "Jesus, Will. Why didn't you tell anyone?"

I raked my hand through my hair. "What would it have changed? I was an asshole when I was a kid. I broke the heart of the only girl who ever meant something to me. So, I'm trying to do it right this time."

"I can see that."

I clicked my tongue. "I don't know why the girls are fighting, Bryce. Why don't you just ask Willow?"

His voice dropped to a whisper. "Sh-sh-sh-sh. Willow's talking to Luna on the phone right now."

I held my breath, waiting on pins and needles for anything that Bryce might've been able to tell me.

"Holy shit," he hissed.

My ears perked up. "What? What is it?"

"No way."

"Bryce, come on. Spill the beans."

He sighed. "No fucking wonder."

"Bryce!"

He hissed at me. "All right, all right. Sorry. Hold on."

I heard him shuffling around before a door closed on his end.

"So?" I asked.

Bryce cleared his throat. "I know what's happening with Sadie? Just heard Willow and Luna talking about it."

"Well...!?"

"From what I heard? It sounded like Sadie's landlord is evicting her, or something like that?"

I blinked. "That doesn't sound right. Sadie being evicted?"

"I'm still not completely sure. Willow said something about Sadie having to move out because of something her landlord did."

My heart stopped in my chest. "You're a genius, you know that?"

"Huh?"

"Remind me to thank you later!"

"Wait, what did I do?"

I shot up from my chair. "I gotta go. We'll talk later. Bye!"

"Will, wai--."

I hung up the phone and felt a surge of life rush through my muscles. That's it. That's what I could give Sadie. If she had to move out of her place with all of those animals, I could give her that.

I could give her a place to go.

I drew in deep breaths through my nose and tried to get my mind to calm down. Excitement took over my entire body, but I knew I had to stay calm. I didn't want to bombard her all at once with this information, especially because of how I'd come across it. So, I forced myself to pull up a text message to Sadie instead of calling her.

Me: You free sometime this week? I'd love to see you.

I watched the screen on my phone and smiled when those three little dots started dancing around.

Sadie: I'm pretty busy with some things that have dropped in my lap. Raincheck?

My fingers flew across the screen as I wiggled my way into the door she left open for me.

Me: You know, that grapevine you and the girls love so much doesn't just talk about my life. What if I told you I had a way to help out?

I expected to see those little dots dancing furiously across the screen. But, there was nothing. I stared at my phone for a full five minutes before I relegated myself to a shower. I mean, sure, it was Saturday and all that. But, I didn't want to spend the day sitting in my own filth.

However, once I got out of the shower, I had a text waiting for me.

Sadie: When would you like to meet up? Mornings are rough for me, but anytime after lunch should be okay.

"Bingo," I murmured.

And as a massive smile crossed my face, my damp fingers plucked out one last message to send off to her. The message that would, hopefully, seal our fate.

As well as put an end to this miserable situation Sadie had found herself in.

Me: How does Friday evening sound? You could come over around four or five, and we can cook dinner here.

Sadie: Sounds perfect. See you then.

❧ 15 ❧

Sadie

As I made my way to Will's place, I shook my head. I didn't know whether to be upset, feel lost, or be confused. The fact that people were already gossiping about me constantly made me infuriated. But the fact that I wasn't going to have anywhere to put myself or my animals in a few weeks made me feel alone and helpless. And to make matters worse, I had no idea what the hell Will had planned for tonight.

I had a feeling it wasn't good, though.

Nonetheless, I needed to get out of my place for a little while. I needed a distraction, and Will was certainly that. So, I'd been looking forward to this surprise little outing all week. I had a cheap bottle of wine sitting in the passenger seat,

along with fruits I picked up from the store and some chocolate dip to heat up in the microwave. But, other than that, I
was flying blind with tonight.

Which felt kind of exciting, in a weird 'I don't want to
have to kill my ex' kind of way.

I made my way down side roads and back roads until I
finally found the gravel shoot-off that led straight through the
woods to Will's place. And when I parked my truck right next
to his, I grabbed my things to head for the door. I drew in
deep breaths as I walked up the stairs. I clutched the bottle of
wine tightly before I knocked my knuckles softly against the
door.

However, when Will opened up, I couldn't take my eyes
off him.

"Hey there, beautiful," he said with a grin.

He had on a pair of tailored suit pants that fit him like a
glove, accenting his long legs and his strong, chiseled thighs.
The button-front shirt he wore was wrinkled from a long
day's work, and the sleeves were rolled up to showcase the
veins trickling up his forearms. And with his tie loosened, the
only thing I wanted to do was shove him back to his bedroom
and have my way with him.

But, I settled for clearing my throat. "You look nice. A
special occasion."

He chuckled as he looked down. "I actually just got back
in from work about half an hour ago. And I'm already eyeing
that bottle of wine you've got in your hand."

I held it out for him. "Then, by all means, let's unwind."

He took it from me. "I like the sound of that."

I saw things sitting out on the counter for dinner as he let me inside. He took the bag of treats from me and promptly stuck them in the fridge. Then I watched as he effortlessly uncorked the bottle of wine. I didn't know whether I was more entranced by his fluid movements or by the wine blubbing itself into a long-stemmed glass.

Nonetheless, I sat down at the kitchen table so I could help take a load off my wobbling legs.

"So, I was thinking steak and vegetables for dinner," Will said as he brought me a glass of wine.

He sat down in front of me, and I felt his feet place themselves against my own. And that small amount of body heat radiating from him sent my heart fluttering.

Stay calm. Stay cool. Stay collected. He's just a man—nothing else.

"Sounds good to me," I said.

I sipped my wine as I watched Will's eyes dance along my body. He was studying me, but I couldn't figure out why. I didn't mind, though. The wine was helping to wash away the shock of being in his presence again.

Because apparently, my mind still hadn't wrapped around the fact that I was seeing him regularly after all this time.

Will drew in a curt breath. "I might as well go ahead and get it out of the way, so if there's fighting, it won't spoil dinner."

I blinked. "Sounds like I'm going to need a taller glass of wine for this."

He reached for the bottle. "I can top you off if you want."

I giggled. "You go right on ahead."

I watched as he filled my wine glass all the way to the top before doing the same with his.

"Long day?" I asked.

He chugged half of his glass down. "Long week. You?"

I rolled my eyes. "Don't even ask."

"All right, then I will: is it true that you have to be out of your place soon?"

I blinked. "Come again?"

He sighed. "I heard a rumor that your landlord is evicting you? Or something like that?"

"I pay my bills, Will. I'm not being evicted."

"I'm just trying to clarify things. I know how you hate rumors."

I shook my head. "Yeah, and I hate people talking about me behind my fucking back."

His eyebrows rose. "Right. Well, I kind of need to know if that's true or not."

"And why's that?"

"Because your answer--which I hope is honest--dictates my next series of questions."

I narrowed my eyes. "Let's just say the rumor's true. Let's say, hypothetically speaking, that my landlord is selling the place. Why do you ask?"

He took another long pull from his wine. He was nervous--that much could be seen. But for what, I wasn't sure.

Will licked his lips. "Look, I know you're upset--."

I held up my hand to interrupt him. "I'm upset, but not at the reason you think."

He paused. "Then, why are you upset?"

I heaved a heavy sigh. "I don't like it when people make speculations about my life because, sometimes, it has a tendency to reveal the fact that people believe my life is more adventurous and entertaining than it really is. I don't like rumors because that's how drama starts and this town is bad for it."

"I completely understand that."

"I know you do. I just--."

I closed my eyes to gather my thoughts before I spit the words out.

"I don't like the fact that you know something I didn't tell you myself."

My eyes slowly opened, and I found Will grinning at me.

"What?" I asked.

He shrugged. "Nothing. You're just--so much like I remembered, yet not at all at the same time."

I giggled softly. "Yeah, I could say the same about you."

His grin grew into a smile. "I feel like you need a safe space to say some things without the fear of someone judging you or getting upset."

"You were always good at giving me those spaces."

"Why don't we have one now, then?"

I snickered. "Not if we both want to eat tonight."

He chuckled. "Then, let's just tackle this most recent

thing. You know, this hypothetical scenario that might not be so hypothetical?"

I swallowed hard. "Safe space?"

He nodded. "Of course."

I drew in a deep breath. "Will, we've been living in the same town together for a while now. But, all of a sudden, it feels like the entire world is working against me to push me into your orbit."

"And... you don't like that."

I took another sip of my wine. "Part of me does wish the universe would stop."

"Do I smell a 'but' coming on?"

I snickered. "But... a very small part of me--and I mean very small--has always missed you and hopes that the universe won't stop, either."

He leaned forward. "Safe space for me, then?"

"Sure. Of course. Go ahead."

He reached out and took my hand from across the table. "I brought you over here tonight and wanted to cook you dinner so you could get another good look at this place and the space it has to offer you and your animals."

I paused. "Why?"

"Because I have intentions of asking you to move in with me and bring your animals here."

I wasn't sure I heard him right. "Come again?"

He grinned, but this time it wasn't devious. "Sadie, you need a place to go where you can be free to roam and take your animals with you. I can give you that. You can stay in my bedroom, or the guest bedroom. Whichever works for you. This cabin has plenty enough space for two people, and I've got five acres of land for the animals to roam. We can set up a training space right here off the front yard or something like that. You can help me with the garden. Hell, we could make a bigger garden with the two of us working at it. And it'll provide you with everything you need until you find a space you want to call your own."

I blinked. "You're being serious."

"As a heart attack, Sadiebee."

I pulled my hand quickly away from his. "What's in it for you?"

I blurted the words out so quickly I hadn't had a chance to consider them, or their impact. And when I saw Will's eye twitch, I knew I had come on too strong.

"That isn't what I meant. What I meant to ask is--."

He held up his hand. "It's okay. Given our past history, you have every right to ask that."

I puffed my cheeks out with a sigh. "I'm so sorry. I didn't mean t--."

"What's in it for me is that I get to see you more often. We get to have more dinners like this. I get to keep an eye on you and make sure you've got everything you need, and I get to interject when I feel you aren't taking care of yourself so I can help you do it myself. Plus, it'll be a little less effort on my part to spend time with you, in general."

I heard him saying all of the right things, but I still felt wary about the situation.

"How much would rent cost me?" I asked.

He scoffed. "You aren't paying rent, Sadie."

My mouth ran away with me again. "Oh? Because I can pay you with sex?"

The heat behind his eyes took over his face as our stares locked together. And when he slowly stood to his feet, my gaze followed him. I watched him come around the table and crouch in front of me as if he were about to propose. And as he took his hand in mine, his eyes softened into something akin to understanding.

"If this is what you really think of me, Sadie, then I don't know why in the absolute hell you've been coming over to spend time with me in the first place. Because the person you have painted in your mind sounds like an absolutely insufferable asshole, and you deserve so much better than that."

Then, I watched him get up from the floor and head into the kitchen to turn on the stove. Readying himself to cook us dinner, despite the royal bitch I had just been to him.

He really has changed.

And now, it was me who didn't deserve him.

❧ 16 ❧

Will

I swiveled around in my office chair as my brother came through my office door. "Bryce, can I ask you a question?"

He paused. "Uh, sure? I was just coming by to drop off this paperwork."

"You had coffee yet this morning?"

He whistled softly. "One of those kinds of talks, huh?"

I swiveled back around. "Close the door. It'll only take a second."

It had been four days since I'd put that offer on the table for Sadie to move in with me, and I hadn't heard a peep out of her since. So, I had to assume she wasn't going to take me up on that offer. And I knew why. I knew it was because of my reputation around town. I just didn't realize it had gotten that bad.

"What's on your mind?" Bryce asked.

I finished what I was typing before I swiveled back around. "Is my reputation around town with women really that bad?"

His eyes widened. "Uh, what? Why do you ask?"

I sighed. "So, that's a 'yes.'"

"Wait, wait, wait. Where the hell is this coming from?"

"Does everyone really think I'm just some playboy that tears through women because that's just what I do, supposedly?"

He shrugged. "Well, I mean..."

My eyebrows rose. "You know that's not who I am, right?"

"Honestly?"

"Yes. Honestly."

He shook his head. "You've always owned it, you know? The women. The one night stands. The club-hopping out of town and expensive dinners that come with certain expectations."

"But, is that really all this place sees when they look at me? Just some guy going through women like people go through ice cream flavors?"

He folded his arms over his chest. "Why are you worrying about this now? What's happened?"

I shrugged. "Just a bit pissed off is all."

"Oh, no-no, no-no. It's much more than that. Spill, Will. What's going on?"

"Really, Bryce. I'm good. Just kind of coming to terms with things."

"Like the fact that you're falling for Sadie again?"

I scoffed. "Idiot. I never stopped falling for the woman because I never stopped loving her."

Silence fell across my office as my brother's face paled. I shook my head and turned back around to my computer, ready to wrap up this conversation. It made me sick to my stomach. No wonder Sadie didn't want to move in with me. She probably thought I'd parade women around like fucking candy while she was living there.

"I'm such an idiot," I whispered to myself.

"You're not an idiot," Bryce said.

I shrugged. "Feel like one."

He rolled next to me in his chair. "Look, you have to admit that your actions over the past few years haven't even sort of alluded to the fact that you were still in love with Sadie. You see that, right?"

I shook my head. "I can't deal with the loneliness, all right?"

My brother put his hand on top of mine to get me to stop typing. "If we're going to have this conversation, then let's have it when we're both at full attention. Okay?"

I slowly looked over at him. "I can't deal with the loneliness and with the emptiness of that cabin. I've never been able to. So, yeah. Other women were company for a night or two. But, after I woke up and realized they weren't Sadie? I had to get them to go, by any means necessary."

Bryce searched my eyes. "Holy shit, you're being serious."

I slumped against my chair. "I've never been so damn serious about anything in all my life."

He sighed. "Fucking hell."

I chuckled. "Right?"

"Okay, okay, okay. So, has something happened with you and Sadie lately? Have you told her any of this?"

"Probably more than I should have, but yeah."

"Did she call you out on any of this? Is that why you're asking me?"

I slid my hand through my hair. "I might have done a bit more than that."

He paused. "What did you do?"

I rolled my eyes. "I offered for her and her animals to come to stay with me at my place since she's about to get thrown out of the place she's renting now."

Bryce stayed so silent that I spun my chair to face him. And when I saw the utter shock on his face, it hit me.

"Oh, fuck," I murmured.

He scoffed. "Yeah. It's clicking now?"

I stood to my feet. "Oh, fuck. Oh, shit."

"Yeah, dude."

My eyes widened. "I asked her to fucking move in with me."

"Yep."

I spun around on my heels. "No wonder she freaked the fuck out."

"It's a big thing, asking someone to move in."

"I-I-I--don't know why I didn't see it. I mean, it's something she needs, right? And I've got the space. A guest bedroom and a bathroom not being used. An entire basement that has nothing in it. Five acres for her animals. I mean, it just seemed like the logical conclusion."

He chuckled. "You really still care about her, don't you?"

I turned to face him. "More than you could possibly imagine."

A knock came at my office door before Bart's voice sounded. "Uh, you guys done? Or do I have to keep waiting?"

I snickered. "Come on in, Bart."

He eased my door open. "Am I interrupting something?"

Bryce pointed. "Can I tell him?"

I shrugged. "Might as well. I need as many people on my side as I can get right now."

Bart paused. "Uh, tell me what?"

Bryce grinned. "Will's still in love with Sadie. Never stopped, apparently."

Bart closed the door behind him. "Oh, that? Yeah, I knew that."

Bryce and I spoke in unison. "You what?"

Bart snickered. "Oh, come on. The way you always stare at her? The stupid way you try to impress her before you realize she's not even watching you? Dude. I'm your brother."

Bryce's face fell. "That doesn't mean you're a genius."

Bart shrugged. "Nope, just a brother."

I blinked. "I guess it's a DNA thing."

Bart grinned devilishly. "Luna and I are talking a bit. She's called me over the past few nights just to rant about things. That was one of them. And besides, I heard some of your conversation while I was waiting for you guys to open the door."

Bryce suppressed his laughter. "You're in such shit, Will. It's wonderful."

I flopped back down into my chair. "I hate my life."

Bart pulled up a chair of his own. "Ah, quit being so dramatic. So, she didn't say 'yes' yet. You fucking asked the girl to move in with you. That's going to take time for her to sift through."

Bryce pointed at me. "You know, it didn't even hit him that he had asked her to move in...which actually meant *dwell* with him...until a few minutes ago, right?"

Bart blinked. "What?"

I waved my hand in the air. "Yeah, yeah, yeah. I'm an idiot. We get that."

Bart leaned forward. "How does 'move in with me' not equate in your mind to someone moving in?"

I glared at him. "I just wanted to give her a practical gift, all right? Give her a place to go so she can take something off her plate."

Bart smiled. "Hell of a gift there, brother."

My head fell back. "I need to get back to work."

Bart patted my knee. "A shred of advice from the youngest?"

I closed my eyes. "What?"

"If you're really that serious about Sadie, then tell her how you feel."

My eyes slowly opened. "Believe it or not, I already did that."

Bryce's face fell flat. "You told Sadie that you still loved her?"

I nodded slowly. "Yep."

Bart narrowed his eyes. "At the same time, you asked her to move in?"

I closed one of my eyes, remembering back to the conversation. "It's a bit more convoluted than that, but essentially yes."

And before either of my brothers could respond, I felt my phone vibrating in my pocket. So, I pulled it out and checked to see who was calling.

But, I came face to face with a text message from Sadie.

"What's wrong?" Bryce asked.

Bart placed his hand on my forearm. "It's Sadie, isn't it?"

I snickered. "She always knows when her ears are burning for a reason."

Bryce rolled closer to me. "What does it say? Did she message?"

And when I read the message to myself, I almost couldn't believe my eyes.

Sadie: I've given your offer a lot of thought, and I've decided to take you up on it. I have to be out by the end of next month. Would you mind if I moved my stuff in phases? It might make things easier.

Relief washed over me as I turned the text message around to show my brothers. And all together, we broke out in smiles and high fives. I leaped to my feet and hugged my brothers close, clapping their backs and laughing because I couldn't contain the excitement rushing through my veins.

"Congratulations," Bryce said.

"Don't do her wrong this time," Bart warned.

I gripped his shoulders. "I won't. You have my word, all right?"

He smiled. "Good."

Bryce patted my back. "Well, I gotta get out of here and do this thing called 'crunching some numbers for the report Bart needs.' You should try it sometime."

I rolled my eyes. "On it, asshole."

Bart pulled out his phone. "And speaking of ladies, Luna's calling me. I'm going to head back out to my desk and take this."

Bryce chuckled. "Don't say anything, I wouldn't say."

I shrugged. "At least he's left you some wiggle room."

Bart shook his head. "See you guys soon. Drinks this weekend?"

I nodded. "Depends on Sadie's move-in schedule, but I'm in."

Bryce pointed at me. "Let me know if she needs any help. I can help haul boxes or whatever in Willow's SUV in case it's raining."

I sat back down in my chair. "I'll definitely let her know. Thank you."

And as I pivoted back around to my computer, my heart swelled with anticipation. In a few weeks, I'd be living with Sadie. Sharing coffee with her every morning and helping her tend to her animals. We'd be a team, albeit a disjointed one. But, it was a team I was hellbent on keeping together, no matter the effort. Or the cost.

I would do anything to keep Sadie at my side for the rest of our days.

17

Sadie

"Where do you want your food-making stuff?" Will asked.

I rolled my eyes. "Will, seriously. That's not funny anymore."

Bryce chuckled. "I still think it's kind of funny."

I looked up from the box I was taping shut. "It was funny the first three times when I had to tell Will everything goes on the truck. But now?"

Luna walked past me with a box in her hands. "She's right. Now, it's just stupid."

Willow giggled. "Awww, cut the man some slack. He's just trying to take this miserable move and turn it into something fun."

Will snickered. "Miserable? Speak for yourself. I love hauling boxes in a ninety-degree out of season heat-wave?"

Luna grinned. "Sadie."

They all fell apart in laughter as I rolled my eyes. I got the last box taped shut for the move and drew in a deep breath of fresh air. Bart had come by earlier to help load up my animals along with their things to get them settled at Will's cabin, and I was thankful that someone had taken that journey off my plate. It was enough work packing up the house, but having to pack up the animals as well?

I wiped the sweat from my brow. "Luna? Can you tell Bart that he was a lifesaver this morning? I still didn't have a plan to move my menagerie when I woke up."

Luna paused. "What makes you think I can tell him that?"

I looked over at Willow. "So, we're still there, huh?"

Luna furrowed her brow. "What?"

Willow nodded. "Yep, but she'll get there. She always does."

Luna paused. "Get where? Where am I going?"

I fell apart in laughter as Will and Bryce came back into the house. Will scooped up the box I had just taped shut while Bryce started plucking pictures off the wall. I back-tracked into the kitchen to grab a water out of the cooler of drinks Bart brought with him this morning and decided to take myself a bit of a break. It had been a long morning, getting everything ready for the move today. And I needed a few minutes to myself to breathe properly.

And with every breath, I felt more positive about my future.

Everything was going really smoothly with this move, though Will was still trying to get me to move into his bedroom. I wasn't ready for something like that, though. Not with him, at least. In some respects, I felt like things were moving way too quickly. I hadn't had a chance to fully determine if Will was different from the boy that broke my heart. But, he sure as hell kept proving that he was different.

That gave me a lot of peace as I sipped my water.

I was hellbent on staying in the guest room, though. No matter what Will said and no matter what he used to entice me, I made a promise to stand my ground on that. I mean, this situation was only temporary in the first place. Once I found a place of my own to rent that had the land I needed and the barn I wanted, I was out of there.

I didn't want to keep relying on the graciousness of others for the rest of my life.

"Knock knock," Will said.

I whipped my head towards him before the room started to tilt.

"Holy shi..."

Will came up to my side. "You okay?"

I felt like I was on a carousel ride. "Uh, I don't know?"

He took my hand in his. "Here, come sit down. You've probably gotten too hot."

I sat gingerly onto the only chair left in the room. "Thanks."

"You need more water?"

I held up my bottle. "Not sure."

"Have you eaten yet today?"

I furrowed my brow. "Huh?"

He crouched in front of me. "Have you eaten yet today?"

My eyes finally found his after the room stopped moving around me. "Why are you asking me these questions?"

He blinked. "Because I'm worried about you?"

It felt like I had stepped into an alternative universe. I'd never seen Will like this, asking all of these questions and worried about how I was feeling. I studied his face and saw the genuine concern behind his eyes and the worried wrinkle of his nose. The way his lips downturned as his eyes danced along my body.

"Here, let me get you some more water," he said.

I tipped my water up to my lips and drained it, thinking maybe I was simply dehydrated. But that didn't help much. Someone plucked the empty bottle from my hand and slid a fresh one against my palm, but then my neck started to cool down substantially.

"Oh, yeah," I groaned.

I felt a cool compress against the nape of my neck before Will's hands gripped my shoulders. He started pressing his thumb into my aching muscles, rolling and rubbing, and ripping from me more moans as I leaned back against the chair. I had just enough energy to crack open the bottle of water and take another sip. But, I was in a completely different universe with how Will was treating me.

"Right there," I whispered.

He kissed the top of my head. "Take another sip of water. I'll keep reminding you."

I sighed. "Thank you."

"Of course. Just don't try to push yourself too much today. You've got us helping for a reason."

Willow's voice filtered down the hallway. "You two okay in there?"

Will called back. "Yep! Sadie just needs a break. We'll be out in a second."

I drew in a deep breath through my nose. "This feels so good. Thank you, Will."

He kissed the top of my head again. "Like I said, just don't push yourself too much. I want you to sit here and finish that bottle of water. I'm going to go help Bryce get the rest of the knick-knacks packed up."

He gave my shoulders one last nice rub before he fell away from me, and my knee-jerk reaction was to reach out for him. To pull him back. His touch felt so good, and him doting on me made me feel important, and I wasn't ready to give that up. Not just yet. But, I needed to sit for a little while. My knees felt weak, and my head still felt as if it were spinning, and the last thing I needed to do was hurt myself during the move.

So, I did as he asked.

"Well, that was interesting," Luna said.

I opened my eyes and saw her sitting on the floor in front of me.

"How long have you been there?" I asked.

She smiled. "Long enough."

I took a long pull from my water. "I never really took Will for the caretaker type, you know."

She giggled. "Trust me, none of us do."

"I mean, even when we were dating back in high school, he was never quite like this. It's almost like he's a--."

She smiled. "Completely different person?"

What did you just learn about judging people? No one is perfect.

And as the sentiment crossed my mind, a smile crept across my cheeks.

"What?" Luna asked.

I finished my water. "Nothing. Just thinking about something."

She scooted closer to me. "Whatcha thinking about?"

I peeked down the hallway and caught Will smiling at me. He waved at me, and I waved back, feeling my heart skipping multiple beats at a time. Just like that couple at the rodeo, I'd caught Will at a bad time in his life. And, just like that couple at the rodeo, I had judged him too harshly and for much too long. He'd done nothing but prove to me, over and over, that he really was different. That he wanted to continue being different than he was before.

So, who was I to question that?

Luna stood. "You feeling any better?"

I turned to face her. "Honestly? Not quite."

She paused. "You sure you're okay? Maybe I should take you to the cabin so you can lay down."

I slowly stood to my feet. "I'll be okay as long as I don't haul anything else. I don't know, I've just got this faint feeling that I can't shake."

"Have you eaten anything since breakfast?"

I paused. "Maybe that's it."

Luna snapped. "Bingo. I'm going to run and get you something to snack on."

Bryce poked his head into the kitchen. "Did someone say 'snacks'?"

Willow soon followed after him. "I mean, I wouldn't mind a snack."

Will rushed down the hallway. "What kind of snack?"

I barked with laughter. "Luna's going to run out and get us all something to munch on before we take this stuff over to the cabin."

Luna pointed at me. "Actually, I was going to raid Bryce and Willow's kitchen, so maybe we all head over to the cabin, and I'll meet you guys there with a late lunch?"

Will slid his arm around my waist. "Sounds like a plan to me. Sadie?"

All eyes were on me as I leaned my head against his chest. "Sounds like a good plan."

Luna clapped her hands. "Great! I'll see you guys over there in, say, forty-five minutes?"

I looked up at Will. "That sound good?"

He smiled down at me. "Sounds perfect."

I gave my small home one last look from top to bottom,

then we all headed out to our respective vehicles. The sun hung high in the sky, and it quickly curdled the water in my stomach. And trust me, it sounds as odd as it felt. My stomach folded over onto itself, and sweat quickly dripped down my neck. I leaned heavily against Will, feeling my legs quickly giving out.

We didn't even make it to his truck before he had to scoop me into his arms.

"Shit," I hissed.

He picked me up against his chest. "All right. That's it. You're going to see a doctor."

"Will, I--."

He opened the truck door. "And I'm not taking 'no' for an answer. Something's wrong. Hey, Bryce!"

"Yeah!?"

"I have to get Sadie to a doctor! Can you get the moving truck to the cabin!?"

I heard someone running over. "What's wrong? Sadie, what's going on?"

The worry in Willow's voice worried me as Will slid me into the passenger seat.

"I don't know what's wrong. I just--I can't walk. I don't know," I murmured.

Will cleared his throat. "You guys are more than welcome to come, but she isn't doing anything else until a doctor sees her."

Bryce trotted up. "I'll get the SUV to the cabin. Then, I'll grab Luna and head that way."

Willow rubbed my leg. "And I'll hitch a ride with you guys if that's okay?"

I nodded slowly. "Please."

Everything kind of moved in a blur as we all broke off with the new plan. I felt helpless with everything going on, but I also felt kind of bad. I mean, I worked in the heat all the time. Rodeo season was spring, summer, and the first two weeks of fall. And it got blazing hot during those months in Conroe. This move should've been easy as pie.

So, why the hell did I feel like such shit after only three hours of work?

The second we pulled into the doctor's office, everything happened in fast-forward. Before I knew it, I had a doctor drawing blood and another one looking down my throat and yet another one testing my reflexes. I felt invaded from all sides, but I felt so weak in my bones that I couldn't even speak up enough to tell them to back off.

"Willow?" I asked weakly.

Will brushed my hair back. "They're all out in the lobby waiting for us, okay?"

I swallowed hard. "What if it's something serious, Will?"

He gazed into my eyes. "We'll tackle it together then, okay?"

I sniffled. "Promise?"

He kissed my forehead. "Promise, promise."

Worry rushed through my veins, and the waiting was the worst. Everything seemed to happen at double the speed until we had to wait for results. Then, everything slowed down to half speed. I wanted to get this over with. I wanted to know what was wrong with me. Because if there was something I needed to fix, then I needed to fix it as quickly as possible.

After all, the training season for my younger animals started in two weeks.

"All right! I have your test results."

I slowly looked over at a woman in a white coat who soared into the room with a clipboard in her hands.

"What's going on?" I asked softly.

The doctor flipped through papers. "Well, we checked your blood sugar, fluid levels, organ functions, and cholesterol. Everything looks fine there. But, when we tested your hormones, I found them to be a bit skewed."

Will swallowed hard. "How skewed?"

I slowly sat up. "Yeah, doctor. How skewed?"

She smiled. "Congratulations, you two."

I blinked. "On what?"

The doctor faltered. "You're pregnant, Miss Sadie. Congratulations!"

And as my eyes slowly drifted over to Will, I watched his skin practically go translucent from the blood that drained from his face.

❦ 18 ❦

Will

*Y*ou're pregnant, Miss Sadie. Congratulations.

My lips ran away from me. "Not possible."

Sadie sighed. "What?"

I shook my head. "That's--that's not possible."

The doctor giggled. "Well, it kind of is. Especially if you've been having unprotected sex."

Sadie shook her head. "Yeah, Will. It's not like we used protection or anything."

I reached out for the clipboard. "Let me see."

Sadie snickered. "Seriously?"

I looked over my shoulder at her. "I want to see it with my own eyes."

I knew she'd be pissed at me for it, but that was literally

impossible. I felt the blood drain away completely from my face as my heart started racing. The doctor handed me the clipboard, and I saw the results right there on paper. Highlighted, circled in bold red, and practically screaming at me.

Holy shit, my Sadie was pregnant.

The doctor started rattling off. "By your hCG levels, I'd suggest you're right there at the beginning stages. Four or five weeks tops."

Sadie whispered. "That lines up."

I shook my head slowly. "That--i-i-it--."

The doctor continued her spiel. "I'll go ahead and get an ultrasound machine in here to confirm my diagnosis, but your hCG levels are as high as they can be for where you are right now in your pregnancy. The fetus is very strong, and I'm pretty sure we'll hear that as well in the heartbeat."

Sadie paused. "Heartbeat?"

I looked up from the clipboard and found the doctor smiling. I felt like I had stepped into an alternative timeline. One straight out of my fucking nightmares.

"I had a vasectomy!" I blurted out.

The entire room stilled, and all eyes were on me.

"You what?" Sadie asked.

I looked over at her. "That's why I never bothered with protection for us. I had a vasectomy about a year ago now. It's not physically possible for you to be pregnant."

Sadie scoffed. "Well, I haven't been with anyone else."

I took her hand. "No, no, no, no. That's not what I'm saying."

She glared at me. "Good."

The doctor cleared her throat. "Well, I can certainly re-run the test, but this is as positive of a test as you can get. Mr. Remington, I'll need you to provide me the information about the doctor that did your vasectomy. I'll need to pull those medical records. And Miss Sadie?"

I watched her lifelessly turn her head. "Yeah?"

The doctor nodded. "I'll re-run the test. Do you mind giving me another blood sample?"

There was something in her face I couldn't read, but it wasn't good. It almost seemed like a mixture of disappointment and fear. But, neither of those made sense. Why would Sadie be disappointed? I mean, I knew she wanted children, but surely not right now. And what was there to be afraid about? The tests were wrong, that's all.

Wait, Sadie still wants children.

Which was something I couldn't give her.

And now, I understood the disappointment and fear behind her stare.

"Oh, boy," I murmured.

The doctor finally broke the tension. "Mr. Remington?"

I snapped my head in her direction. "Yes?"

"May I ask you a few questions about your vasectomy?"

I nodded mindlessly. "Yeah. Sure."

The doctor plucked a pen from her breast pocket. "Were there any complications?"

I shook my head. "Not that I can recall, no."

"Was it a hard recuperation?"

"Not one bit. I was down for less than forty-eight hours, then I was back traveling."

She peeked up at me. "Traveling?"

I nodded. "Yes. For my family's company."

"Uh-huh. And did you make time for your follow-up appointments?"

I felt my gut settle at my toes. "Appointments? As in, more than one?"

The doctor stared at me. "After a vasectomy, a man has at least four scheduled appointments to test sperm content in the semen. And if there's still a sperm content after those four scheduled appointments, then more are scheduled until there's no sperm count at all to be registered."

The room tilted around me. "Are you--are you serious?"

Sadie placed her hand on my shoulder. "Will, look at me."

My eyes panned over to her. "I only did one follow-up."

She nodded softly. "I know."

I shook my head. "I only thought it was one follow-up."

She sighed heavily. "I know you did."

I swallowed hard. "Sadie, I'm so sorry. If I had known--."

She turned away from me quickly. "We'll pass on the ultrasound for today, but thank you."

It felt like someone had tossed me into a vat of jello and asked me to walk around as if nothing had happened. It felt like I couldn't draw in a deep breath, or like someone was sitting on my shoulders. I eased myself into a chair as the doctor slipped out of the room, leaving Sadie and me alone with our silent thoughts.

Then, she asked the one question that gutted me completely. "You don't want children, do you?"

I swallowed hard. "Sadie, I--."

She slid off the exam table. "It's a simple 'yes' or 'no' question."

I reached out for her hand. "It really isn't."

She slipped away, refusing to touch me. "Just answer it, please."

My head fell back with frustration. "When I saw everything that happened between Bryce and his ex, I just thought--."

"--you'd have a vasectomy so you wouldn't get one of your one-night stands pregnant and feel the need to settle down with her forever?"

My head snapped back upright. "It's not quite like that."

Sadie wrapped her arms around her body. "Then, what's it like? Because from what I know, Bryce did the honorable thing. And it sounds like you took the shitty way out so you'd never have to be caught dead doing anything honorable."

I sprang to my feet. "That's not what happened in my head, and you know it. Why in the world are you still trying to paint me like the immature, asshole kid I was when we were teenagers?"

Her eyes watered over. "Because during all of this, it never once occurred to you to tell me that you didn't want children."

I paused. "Is that information I needed to be up front

with? Because the last time I checked, we weren't in a relationship."

The second those words flew out of my mouth, I knew I'd buried myself. The pain that washed over Sadie's face was unspeakable, and it knocked the air out of my lungs.

"Sadie, that isn't what--."

She held up her hand. "Get away from me."

I took a step toward her. "Sadie, please. What I was trying to say is--."

She reached for the doorknob. "Oh, you made that very clear."

I gripped her arm. "No, no. You're reading way too much into my words. Just hear me out."

She wrenched away from me. "Get your hands off me, William."

I froze at the sound of my full name. Sadie never called me that unless she was spitfire angry with me. I didn't want to let her go, though. Not until I explained myself. Not until I had said my piece. Because I knew if she just heard me out, this wouldn't be such a big deal.

Well, mostly.

"I have to go," she breathed.

I didn't know what to do. "Come on. Let's go home."

She held her finger up at me. "Let's get one thing straight: your cabin is not my home. It's a stopping point. A transition. And I won't move into your room or plant roots with you in that place, is that understood?"

My heart shattered in my chest. "Understood."

"Good. Now, I'm going to go get some water and then we need to go back to the cabin. We still have a lot to get done today."

"You need to rest. We can handle it."

She glared up at me. "You don't want kids, so you don't get to dictate what I do while I'm pregnant with one. Got it?"

I nodded curtly. "Got it."

For one split second, she afforded me the deepest look into her eyes I'd ever had the pleasure of experiencing. And after digging through all of the anger and the shock and the frustration, there was that scared little girl I fell in love with all those years ago. Sadie was terrified, and I knew exactly how she felt. Neither of us was prepared for a child.

Then again, who was ever prepared for something like that?

Willow and Bryce weren't.

"Do you want to tell the--?"

Sadie turned away from me. "We tell no one until I know what I'm going to do."

I blinked. "What does that mean?"

She clicked her tongue. "Nothing, since you don't want kids."

As she made her way out of the room, I felt every ounce of happiness I had accrued over the past weeks draining from my body. I felt it pooling beneath me and evaporating into the clouds, never to be seen again. I watched as Sadie disappeared around the corner. I heard her sniffling down the hallway. And as the doctor came back into the room, her eyes went from excited to sympathetic.

"Give her some time," the doctor said.

I nodded mindlessly. "Yeah, that doesn't work with her."

"Why not?"

Because she still thinks I'm that guy. "Just a hunch."

I made my exit out of the room as the reality of our situation dawned on me. Had Sadie and I already met our end before we could even get something off the ground? The thought made me sick to my stomach. We hadn't even gotten her settled into my place, and already lines were being drawn in the sand. I walked into the waiting room and saw the girls embracing. Bart and Bryce were there, and they rushed over to my side the second I entered the room.

I couldn't stop staring at Sadie, though.

I couldn't stop watching her as she cried against Willow's shoulder.

"What's going on?" Bryce asked.

Bart put his hands on his hips. "Sadie says it's dehydration and exhaustion. But, why would she be crying over that?"

I shook my head slowly. "I'm honestly, not sure."

The girls ushered Sadie out of the room, and I did the same with my brothers. But, I didn't even get through the door before the doctor stopped me.

"Mr. Remington!"

I turned around. "Yeah, doc?"

She crooked her finger at me, and I rolled my eyes before making my way back to her.

"Yes?" I murmured.

She handed me a clipboard. "I called your surgeon. I want to get you in here to run sperm count tests. We need to figure out where your levels are and how to get them down to zero, okay?"

I mindlessly signed off on the tests. "Whenever you schedule it, I'll come in."

She took the clipboard from me. "Wonderful. I'll call you before the day is out to get your first appointment scheduled."

"Can I ask you something?"

She nodded. "Sure. Go ahead."

I took a moment to gather my thoughts. "Vasectomies are reversible, right?"

She smiled softly. "Yes, sir. They are."

"And... how long is that surgery, if I decide to reverse it?"

Her smile grew. "No longer than the one you've already had."

I turned to face my brothers. "Thank you, doctor, for everything you did today for Sadie."

She patted my back. "I'll call you this afternoon and get you in here for an appointment. Oh, and here. She's going to need this."

I felt something press against my palm, and when I looked down, I saw it was a prescription for Sadie's prenatal vitamins. I quickly shoved it into my pocket as I felt my brother's prying eyes raking up and down my form. I held my head high as I walked outside, knowing damn good and well I'd be assaulted with questions the second my brothers got me alone.

But for now, my focus was on Sadie.

And how the hell to fix the massive hole I dug back there in that office.

I wasn't sure if the girls knew, especially since they were still smiling at me and treating me to sympathetic hugs and well wishes. And while I wanted to ask Sadie if she had any plans to tell the girls, I also knew better than to keep poking at a bear when it was angry. So, I slipped behind the wheel of my truck and kept my eyes forward, even though I wanted to steal glances at the beautiful woman sitting in my passenger's seat.

At this point, I didn't know which one of us was in the right or in the wrong, or even if we stood a chance at getting through this mess I had somehow created. But, I knew one thing was for certain, no matter what came of Sadie and myself.

If she decided to have this baby, I'd help in any way possible.

"Sadie?" I asked softly.

She sniffled. "I just can't right now, okay?"

I swallowed hard. "Then, can you just listen?"

She sighed. "Whatever. Sure. It's not like I have a choice."

I peeked at her. "You do have a choice. I'm just hoping you'll choose to let me talk."

Her gaze fell out the windshield. "Fine."

It's better than nothing. "Back there in the office, I handled it completely wrong."

She scoffed. "You think?"

"Just let me finish, please?"

She folded her hands in her lap. "Sorry."

"You have no reason to apologize, but I do. I handled that completely wrong, and I'm sorry. I know this is a shock for both of us, but I should have been upfront with you about my vasectomy. Especially since I know how you feel about children."

She shrugged. "Things change. You had no way of knowing."

I came to a stop at a stoplight. "I guess I just want you to know that even though this is a shock and even though this does put us in a weird position, I'm going to help. If you choose to have this child, I'll do whatever I can to help out. Money, or getting you guys a place to live, or getting us a new place to live, or taking over your business so you can recuperate from birth, or--."

"Let's not get ahead of ourselves right now, okay?"

I blinked. "You don't know if you're having the child, do you?"

She shrugged. "Let's just not get ahead of ourselves right now. That's all I'm saying."

And as I pulled off the back road and eased down the gravel pathway towards my cabin, I wasn't sure which one was worse.

Hurting Sadie like I had, or not knowing if she wanted to keep our child.

❧ 19 ❧

Sadie

I felt the bottle of prenatal vitamins staring at me from my bedside table. Will had been in and out of the cabin all day while everyone else unloaded and helped me unpack things.

Late this afternoon, he picked them up and came back with all sorts of brochures on pregnancy that he had surreptitiously slid underneath my pillow. And as I laid there with those vitamins taunting me and those brochures scattered all across my bed, I let my hand settle over my belly.

"I'm pregnant," I whispered.

No matter how many times I said it, it didn't feel any more comfortable. No matter how many times I rubbed my belly, it just didn't seem real. And I kept playing Will's reaction over and over in my head again.

The man had been absolutely petrified.

Tears rushed my eyes as I drew in deep breaths. This should've been such a happy time in my life. For as long as my mind remembered, I'd wanted children. Lots of them, too. So many girls I grew up with wanted careers and condos on the beach and independence. But, me? I wanted that traditional life. I wanted to be a homemaker. I wanted to be barefoot and pregnant in the kitchen with a doting husband with pies baking in the oven.

I also remembered getting teased relentlessly for it as a kid.

It didn't change what I wanted, though. And I never imagined in a million years that my first pregnancy would be more devastating than exciting. I mean, the absolute horror that crossed Will's face whenever the doctor told me I was pregnant spoke volumes.

Actually, that look in his eye was the reason I found myself staring up at the ceiling at midnight.

My stomach started growling, so I decided to try my hand at eating something. I sat up and eased myself off the bed before I padded softly out of the guest room. After all, I didn't want to wake up, Will. The last thing I needed to deal with was his explanations and his apologies.

Not because I wasn't deserving of them, but because they softened me toward him.

And I wasn't done being pissed yet.

"Fancy seeing you here."

I yelped at the sound of Will's voice before cupping my hand over my mouth. My eyes widened as I scanned the room before finding him in the kitchen. The smell of coffee filled the atmosphere, and my mouth began watering. Then, as if he could read my thoughts, Will was standing in front of me with a mug hovering in front of my chest.

"Don't worry. It's decaf," he said.

I took the mug. "Thank you. I appreciate it."

"You, uh, you want to sit?"

I sipped the decaf coffee and groaned with delight. "Oh, yeah."

He chuckled. "Good?"

I nodded. "Very. Thank you."

"Of course. Anything I can do to help, I will."

His hand fell to the small of my back as he guided me over to the couch. I eased myself against the cushions and sank back against the softness of the microfiber as I took another long pull of the creamy decaf coffee. I wanted to ask Will how the hell he knew to make decaf, especially when he wasn't sure I'd be up or anything. But, I swallowed it down and decided that question was for a different day.

Right now? We had a lot we needed to talk about that had nothing to do with what he did and did not know.

I glanced out the window and saw what looked like a storage shed at the corner of the property. I furrowed my brow and squinted my eyes, trying to make sense of the yard in front of me.

It wasn't until Will spoke, though, that I understood what I was looking at.

"The shed is courtesy of Bart."

I looked up at him. "What?"

Will snickered. "When Bart got all of the animals here, he realized I didn't have much space to put their stuff. So, he spent the morning finding a shed to rent and had it hauled out here. All of your feed and tack and things like that are in the shed."

"I owe him a massive 'thank you.'"

"He figured you might say that, so he told me to tell you 'no thanks necessary.'"

I giggled. "I'll still tell him anyway."

"I know you will. It's what makes you wonderful."

I felt my cheeks blush, but I didn't offer up anything else. Will was charming, yes, but I couldn't let his charm get in the way of what we had to do. Compliments would only get him so far at this point, especially with the situation we had been presented with this afternoon.

I finished my mug of coffee in silence before Will scooted closer to me, closing the gap between us on the couch until our thighs touched.

"I'm sorry for how I reacted in the doctor's office today, Sadie."

I set my mug down on the floor. "It's not like I had the best reaction, either."

"But still, it was out of line. I should've kept a cool head in that office, and I didn't."

I barked with bitter laughter. "Well, given the circumstances, it's understandable. I was pretty floored myself."

"I also scheduled an appointment with the doctor today. I have to go back in tomorrow and have my sperm count tested."

I nodded mindlessly. "I'm glad you're finally getting it done."

He took my hand. "I don't need that test to know that child is mine, though. I hope you know that."

And finally, she wrapped her fingers around my hand. "I do. It just hurt a lot when there was the insinuation that this child somehow wasn't yours."

"I never should have made you feel that way. Ever. I should have cleared that shit up in the office right then and there."

"Can I ask you something?"

His thumb smoothed against my skin. "Of course. You can ask me anything."

I looked over at him. "Why did you never schedule those follow-up appointments?"

He shrugged. "I don't know. I mean, I had that first one, and the doctor told me things looked good, so I figured that was that. I guess I didn't really realize what he was doing. I was just so relieved at the time that the vasectomy went well that when the doctor tried scheduling more appointments, I didn't take them seriously."

"That makes sense."

"Plus, a lot of them conflicted with business trips I needed to take. So, my usual response was that I'd contact him when I got back home and just never did."

I slid my hand out of his. "You want to know what's funny, though?"

He paused. "What?"

I shrugged. "I'm not even angry about all of that."

"You're not?"

I shook my head. "No. In fact, you haven't yet touched on why I'm still upset with you."

"I'd really like to know why you're upset, then. If anything, so I can try and make it right."

I gazed into his confused eyes. "I just got the scariest, most fantastic, most terrifying, most beautiful news today, and not once did I feel like you were on my side."

I turned away from Will as I fought back the tears. That really was the only thing I felt truly upset about. After digging through all of the anger and the shock and the audacity I felt at some of the things Will said in that office, it all boiled down to one concept:

The fact that I still felt alone in that place, even though he'd been right there.

"Sadie, I--."

I held up my hand. "This isn't something you can apologize away on a whim, Will."

"I know. I know."

I stood to my feet. "No, you really don't."

I turned to face him, and I watched as helplessness spread across his features.

"Sadie, please."

I shook my head. "Don't beg. It doesn't sound good in your voice. I just--."

I backed away from him until I found myself standing at the window. So, I turned to look out at my animals that had flopped down in the middle of the rich, green grass and made their bed for the night. They all looked so peaceful and so innocent. Almost as if they finally knew they were home.

This place didn't feel like home, though.

It felt more like a prison sentence.

"Sadie?" Will asked softly.

I watched his reflection approach me in the window before I turned around.

"I just need some time, Will. Okay?"

He nodded. "Sure, sure. Of course. You take all the time you need."

My appetite quickly faded away. "I think I'm going to try and go lay down again."

"You sure there isn't anything else you need?"

I blinked back tears. "I just need sleep. It's been a day."

"You're on the verge of crying."

My voice grew heated. "You think I don't know that?"

He closed the distance between us. "I'm not letting you cry alone."

I tried shoving him away. "Not your call."

"Sadie, stop it."

I tried, yet again, to push him away from me. "Will, just let me go to bed."

He gripped my wrists. "Sadie, stop it."

"Will, cut it out. Please!"

"Sadie!"

"Damn it, Will, why can't you just be on my side for once!?"

He wrapped his arms around me and pinned me to the window, and everything fell apart. My body shook so violently it actually worried me as cries of anguish and fear and sadness tore from the back of my throat. My tears tried to drown my cheeks in their rivers as my legs gave out beneath me, sinking both of us to the ground.

And as Will gathered me in his lap, I cried into the crook of his neck.

"I'll always be on your side. I swear it," he whispered.

I sobbed against his skin. "I'm so fucking petrified."

He rocked me softly. "I know. I know. So am I."

"I fucking know you are, you twat."

He chuckled. "But, you aren't doing this alone. Even if you feel that way right now, I'm always going to be here. Okay?"

I gripped his shirt with my hands. "I don't know what to do. What about my business? Where am I going to live?"

He kissed my temple. "We'll work all of that stuff out once we get some sleep."

"I hate you so much sometimes," I whispered.

"Trust me, I hate myself sometimes, too."

It was the most honest admission I'd ever heard fall from his lips, and it broke my heart. I heard the pain in his voice. The disappointment in himself that laced through every letter of his words. I curled as deeply into his body as I could, trying to provide comfort for a heart that was hurting, just like mine. For once, we were on the same page. We might've been feeling that hurt for different reasons, but the feeling and the impact was still the same. And as we sat there together, beneath the window by his fireplace, I realized something.

Despite how terrible this day had been, I still wouldn't have wanted to do it with anyone other than him.

Than Will.

Than the man I had never stopped loving.

"Sadie?"

I looked up into his determined face. "Yeah?"

His eyes met mine. "No matter what it costs me--and no matter what happens--you won't do this alone. Okay?"

I nodded softly. "Okay."

"From this point forward, I'm making it my sole mission to make sure you don't ever feel alone. Because you sure as hell aren't doing this alone. Got it?"

I smiled. "Got it."

He kissed the tip of my nose. "Good."

And for the first time since Will came to my doorstep groveling with flowers and chocolates all those years ago, I actually believed him.

I believed the words falling from his lips.

And they gave me hope.

❧ 20 ❧

Will

My cell phone started ringing, and I jumped. I leaped up from my office desk chair and scrambled to get it out of my pocket, hoping and praying it was the doctor's office.

And it was.

"Doctor Lamberg?"

Her delightful giggle settled against my ears. "Been waiting for my phone call?"

I snickered. "Ever since my appointment yesterday. How do things look?"

She sighed. "Well, they looked about how I expected."

"Which is...?"

"Your sperm count is very low, Mr. Remington. It's actually a bit lower than what we would have expected at this stage of recovery from your surgery."

It killed me to hear the fact that I was still in 'recovery' from a surgery I had over a year ago.

"But...?" I asked.

Dr. Lamberg clicked her tongue. "But, you do still have a sperm count. I want to schedule you another appointment next month to have your levels checked again."

I raked my hand through my hair. "Yeah, yeah, yeah. Of course. Uh, just schedule it and email me, and I'll make it work."

"Sounds good. Expect a confirmation email in your inbox by the end of the day."

"Thank you. I appreciate everything you've done for Sadie and me."

I heard her smile through the phone. "No worries. How are those prenatals doing for her? Do you know?"

I grinned. "She's got a lot more energy now, and she's eating a bit. So, that's good."

"Any reason why she's not eating?"

I shrugged. "Just nauseous. It's kicking her ass. I mean, her butt. It's kicking her butt."

She barked with laughter. "You don't have to be a prude with me, Mr. Remington. I just handled your sperm in order to check its count."

I snickered. "Right, right."

"Well, tell Miss Sadie that ginger helps upset stomachs, but if her nausea gets to a point where she isn't eating at all, that'll require a visit back to me. Just keep tabs on it."

I nodded. "Will do, Doc. Thanks."

"Anytime, Mr. Remington."

I hung up the phone and dropped it aimlessly onto my desk. Holy shit, I still had sperm in my semen. I mean, not that there was any question about it, but having proof? Having a doctor tell me that?

How many other women have I gotten pregnant?

The question slammed into me so hard that I fell back down into my desk chair. I swiveled back toward my computer screen, but I knew I had no hope of ever focusing on work. Between worrying about Sadie and fatherhood looming over my head and getting up in the middle of the night to help Sadie with her hair while she vomited, I felt like I was moving in a foggy haze.

"I can only imagine how she feels," I whispered to myself.

How in the hell was I going to change my entire life to center around a child? I mean, let's face it: my life wasn't conducive for raising a child. I worked a hell of a lot. Traveled even more, too. And when I wasn't traveling, I was either helping my brothers out with something or visiting our parents in Italy. Taking on a child would require a complete one-eighty turnaround from my current lifestyle.

I have to talk to Bryce.

With my older brother now being a father of two, I knew he'd have advice for me—tips and tricks for coping and staying strong for Sadie, like she needed me to. But, Sadie wasn't ready to tell anyone yet.

I couldn't approach my brother until Sadie gave me the okay to do so.

"Fuck!" I exclaimed.

I reached down and turned off the tower to my computer before I started packing up my things. There was no use in me sitting here for three hours and wallowing in my own self-pity when there was a woman back at my cabin that needed me. That needed someone strong at her side. I had better things to be doing than fucking paperwork and planning trips, so I charged out of my office and headed straight for my truck.

Then, less than five minutes later, I inched my way up the gravel driveway.

As I parked in front of the cabin, I saw Sadie out in the yard with the animals. I saw her walking a sheep in a harness around in a circle while holding out a treat for it to follow. I saw her goats feeding on some shrubs at the corner of the property near the north wood-line. I even saw the couple of miniature horses she had galloping up and down the backyard, playing with one another before they started rolling in the grass.

I sat there and watched since she obviously hadn't realized I'd pulled up to the house.

I watched her walk over to the storage shed and pull out feed. And when she started ringing a bell that she reached for in the darkness of that shed, I watched the animals gallivant in her direction. She tossed out feed and sprinkled it about, wearing the biggest smile I'd ever seen her don.

I'd give anything to make her smile like that.

I watched how the sunlight streamed through her gorgeous locks. I watched as her limber, luscious body moved and dipped and bent forward and swayed. She was a vision. An angel that had fallen from heaven to redeem the demons in my soul. She had been wrapped up in a dream and served to me on a silver platter, and I still couldn't get shit right.

I was determined to, though.

I was determined to do right by her *and* our child.

I wasn't sure what I had done in my life to deserve such a scene unfolding before my eyes, but I made a vow to myself at that moment. As I turned off the engine of my truck and leaped out onto the gravel, I promised myself that I'd do everything in my power to keep this family together.

Because that's what we all deserved, in the end.

"Need any help!?" I yelled across the yard.

Sadie whipped her head up, and even from a distance, I saw the surprise in her face.

"Will! Hey!" she called back.

I cupped my hands over my mouth. "Have you eaten!?"

I watched her shake her head, and I sighed.

"I'm gonna make some soup! You in!?"

She gave me a thumbs up. "Lemonade, too!?"

I smiled. "Anything you want!"

She blew me a kiss, and I pretended to catch it and put it in my pocket. I heard her giggles from across the lawn, and it fucking blew me away, how wonderful this all felt. Coming home to Sadie in the yard with the animals. Me, making my way inside to cook us a meal we'd share together. It all felt so domestic and homey. In my eyes, it was the billboard definition of the word 'happiness.'

Damn it, I loved this woman.

I made my way inside and headed straight for the fridge. I pulled out the fresh bag of lemons in one of the bottom drawers and quickly got to work on my homemade lemonade. I wasn't sure why everyone loved it so much. I mean, it was just lemons, some warm water, and two cups of sugar—nothing fancy, nothing spectacular, just a nice lemonade with enough tart to cut through the sweetness.

But, it was my most requested item to bring to cookouts and family gatherings alike.

After getting the lemons and the sugar in the hot water, I set it off to the side. I pulled a pot down from one of the overhead cabinets and put it on the stove, ready to cook us up a massive thing of soup that would be easy for us to reheat in the coming days. Whenever I felt sick to my stomach, soup always helped. It was light and easy to get down, and easy on the throat if it ever came back up.

I just hoped Sadie kept it down. Both for her sake, and for our growing child.

I heard the front door open. "Since when do you come home from work early?"

I chuckled. "Since I've got someone to come home to. Why? You don't like it?"

She giggled as she closed the door. "The opposite, actually. I could kind of get used to it."

I smiled. "Sounds good to me."

She sniffed the air. "Mmmm, I already smell that lemonade."

I started chopping vegetables. "You want a broth base or a creamy base to your soup?"

"Broth, definitely. And carrots. Oh, can you put carrots in there?"

I peered over my shoulder. "I thought the cravings came after the nausea."

She glared playfully at me. "Just put carrots in the damn soup."

"Whatever you want, Angel."

She paused. "Angel?"

I nodded. "You're my angel, at least."

She grinned. "Does this mean you're my little demon?"

My mind completely abandoned the vegetables. "If you'd like me to be."

She sauntered toward me, her hips swaying deeply. "What if this angel wants you to be a bad little boy?"

I felt my cock already stiffening. "That can most certainly be arranged... *Angel.*"

She walked over to me and wrapped her hand up in my loosened tie. And when she stood to her tiptoes, she crashed her lips against my own. My arms cloaked her back, shielding her from the rest of the world as our tongues fell together in a familiar tango they had danced all too much. I growled down the back of her throat. I gripped her voluptuous ass cheeks and hoisted her onto the kitchen island. Her legs spread wondrously for me, and I inched between them, feeling her warmth welcoming me back into the fold.

"My God, you're perfect," I whispered.

Sadie kissed the tip of my nose. "What was that for?"

My eyes slowly opened. "What was what for?"

"That word. Perfect. Why did you say that?"

I blinked. "Because you're perfect. That's why."

"I'm hardly perfect, Will."

"Well, you're perfect for me. That so bad?"

She giggled. "If you kiss me like that every day, not one bit."

I captured her lips one last time, allowing the kiss to linger against my lips. I cupped the back of her head and gripped her hair, feeling her tendrils effortlessly wrap themselves around my skin. I wanted more of her... All of her. Every single bit of her she'd give me.

But, I decided not to push things too quickly.

My forehead fell against hers. "There anything I can help you with outside?"

She shook her head softly. "I'm actually done for the day until they need dinner."

"Well, you let me feed them tonight. I want you resting."

"Will, I can--."

I gripped her chin as my eyes hardened on her gaze. "I'm doing dinner tonight. Okay?"

She nodded softly. "Okay."

I cupped her cheek. "Now, get yourself a glass of ice. This lemonade should be ready for a cool glass."

And the excited smile that spread across her face filled me with more pride than I'd ever felt in my entire life.

Knowing I could still make Sadie smile after all we'd been through in our lives together was the best gift anyone could have ever given me.

21

Sadie

I paced the living room as I waited for the girls to arrive. While I had unresolved issues with Willow, I needed my best friends. I felt lost at sea in a storm I had no control over, and I needed some rational, unbiased thoughts.

Because my heart was all over the place.

The second I heard their cars pull up, I rushed over and ripped the front door open. Willow and Luna bounded up the steps, greeting me with hugs and cheek kisses before I ushered them inside. We all sat around the kitchen table, where I had fresh lemonade and all sorts of snack items sitting out for us to enjoy.

But, when we sat down, all eyes were on me.

"You doing okay, Sadie?" Willow asked.

Luna nodded. "You look a bit pale."

"I mean, I was going to say tired."

"Are you eating? You really should be eating."

I put my hand in the air, stopping their assault of questions. "Luna, how's your father?"

She furrowed her brow tightly. "He's, uh... well, he's doing good. Getting better and not needing me as much. If things keep going like this, I should be back in my place by the end of next month."

I looked over at Willow. "How are you doing? How's Bryce and the kids?"

She paused. "You're scaring me a bit. You've never been one for small talk."

Luna snickered. "Yeah. If anything, you can't stand the stuff."

I shrugged. "Can't a girl learn what's going on in her best friend's worlds?"

They looked at me as if I'd grown a third head. So, I drew in a deep breath and pulled out the big guns.

"Please, guys? Just make things feel normal for a split second?" I asked.

Luna hopped to the forefront first. "Well, I do miss having a life of my own. I never really realized how much work it would be to help my father through a double hip replacement. I'm kind of ready to get back out there and live my life."

Willow nodded. "And the kids are driving me nuts. I mean, I love them, don't get me wrong. But, damn it, they're just a direct extension of their father, and I can't handle it sometimes. I'm actually glad you called because I was going stir crazy in that house today."

We all shared a small moment of laughter before things fell silent again.

"Sadie? What's going on?" Luna asked softly.

My watery gaze met Willow's prying stare. "I owe you an apology. A big one."

She took my hand. "I don't care about that. I care about what's wrong. Because clearly, something's wrong."

I squeezed her hand. "You were right, you know?"

Willow nodded. "I usually am. But what was I right about this time?"

Luna barked with laughter. "That's Willow for you."

I smiled softly. "About Will and I. About me giving him a second chance. You were right. He's not the same person he was all of those years ago, and he did deserve a second chance.

Willow's eyes lit up. "Are you telling me what I think you're telling me?"

Luna leaned forward. "Are you and Will together?"

I'd never been good at finesse or grace. I walked clumsily, I always dropped things, and I'd broken my toes countless times because I never knew where to move my foot some days.

So, I didn't try to have finesse now. "Yes, Will and I are together. But, before you get excited, we're kind of being tossed into the deep end."

Luna narrowed her eyes. "What are you talking about?"

Willow gasped. "Oh, shit."

I nodded slowly. "Yeah."

Willow released my hand and cupped hers over her mouth. "You're kidding."

Luna's eyes darted between us. "What? What!? Someone fill me in already!"

I sighed. "I'm pregnant, Luna."

The entire cabin went silent as Willow's jaw slowly unhinged. It kept falling and falling, moving in tandem with the shock washing over Luna's features. They expressed the shock I felt deep down inside every day I woke up. Every symptom that caught me off-guard and every wave of exhaustion that took me to my knees in the middle of the day shocked me to my core.

I watched the girls look at one another before they both looked back at me. And then, even more questions were unleashed.

"What the hell are you talking about, you're pregnant?" Luna asked.

Willow shook her head. "When? How? How far along are you?"

"When the hell were you two even sleeping together!?"

"Have the two of you talked about this at all?"

"Does Will know?"

"Please tell me you've told him."

I held up my hand again, and they fell silent. "Yes, Will knows."

Willow breathed a sigh of relief. "Well, thank fuck for that."

Luna clicked her tongue. "I'm sorry. But, when the fuck did this happen?"

I swallowed hard. "Uh, a few days ago, I think? That's when we found out?"

Willow shook her head. "Well, you can't be more than a month or two along, right? I mean, you and Will didn't reconnect until..."

Luna and Willow looked at one another before they spoke in unison.

"The barbecue."

I snickered. "Yeah. That little shindig."

Willow looked tentatively over at me. "Look, I'll admit to getting you and Will in one place to see if you two might rekindle something. But, I didn't expect it to go this far this quickly."

I scoffed. "Think about how I feel, then!""

Luna blinked. "Are you happy about this? Is this a... good thing?"

Her question brought silence to my mind as I searched for a way to answer. Because the truth of the matter was, I wasn't certain.

"I don't really know how to answer that question if I'm being honest," I said softly.

Luna nodded. "All right. Let's rephrase, then: could you be happy raising a child with Will?"

My eyes watered with tears, but not the bad kind. "Yes. I could."

Willow smiled. "There's that look."

Luna grinned. "I haven't seen that look in your eye since high school."

Willow giggled. "You still love him, don't you?"

I swallowed hard. "You guys, what if I'm not the only woman he's gotten pregnant?"

Luna paused. "I'm not following."

I pinched the bridge of my nose. "The doctor's appointment, remember? When I wasn't feeling well during the move?"

Willow gasped. "That's when you found out? And you didn't tell us!?"

I glared at her. "Listen to me, okay? Because this part's very important. It's the reason why I can't sleep right now."

Luna scooted her chair closer to me. "Talk to us. What's going on?"

I licked my lips. "In the doctor's office, Will admitted to having a vasectomy."

"What!?" Willow exclaimed.

Luna furrowed her brow. "When?"

I shrugged. "It was apparently around the time that Bryce was going through all of that shit with Patricia. He said he never wanted to find himself in that kind of a situation with a one-night stand, so he got snipped."

Willow held her hand out. "But, obviously, it didn't take?"

I shook my head slowly. "He never did all of the follow-up appointments. So, he's still had a sperm count this entire time when he thought he was fine."

Luna scoffed. "Fucking men."

I snickered. "Right?"

Willow scooted around to my other side. "So, you're afraid Will's got more kids out there with women that didn't come forward about the pregnancy?"

I sighed. "I mean, can you blame me?"

Willow wrapped her arm around my shoulders. "Will was probably careful with all of those other girls. I mean, he's got his moments, sure. But, he's not a complete idiot."

I shook my head. "We didn't use any protection. Who's to say those girls aren't any different?"

Luna giggled. "You know that man has never stopped loving you. Why the hell would he treat other women like he treats you?"

I shot her a look. "That still isn't proof. That doesn't keep me from worrying."

Willow squeezed my shoulder. "Have you told him any of this? What you're so worried about?"

I shrugged. "I can't. I don't know why, I just--I mean, what if we decide to live a public, happy life together, and then women start popping up out of the woodwork claiming their child is Will's? I mean, it's not like the Remington brothers aren't known around town for the one thing a single mother would need the most of."

Willow and Luna answered together. "Money."

I continued with my train of thought. "And I'm not saying that all women are horrible. But, what if these women asked him to step up? To be the father he's trying to be for our child? What would that mean for our life together? For our lives regarding the child I'm currently growing? I mean, what the hell am I supposed to do with that?"

Luna snickered. "Man, we can really get ourselves into some trouble now that we're adults."

Willow barked with laughter. "Ain't that the truth."

I giggled. "Oh, what has happened to us, girls?"

Willow rubbed my back. "We've fallen in love."

Luna held her finger in the air. "Correction: you two have fallen in love. I haven't quite screwed my life up yet."

The three of us fell apart in laughter to try and dispel some of the heaviness of the conversation before silence fell upon us yet again.

As if to return us back to the bleakness of my situation.

"There isn't an answer to my issue, is there?" I asked softly.

Willow sighed. "The answer is to talk to Will about this."

Luna nodded. "Yeah. He needs to know what you're thinking and how you're feeling. He's the one you need to express these concerns to."

"And who knows," Willow said with a shrug, "he might have the same concerns as you."

Luna rubbed my arm. "Which means you wouldn't be alone. And that helps a lot."

I drew in a deep breath. "I know, I know. It's just--there's so much fallout that could come with this situation. And while I know I'm just as responsible as he is for all of this, I'm still so angry at him. Here we are, trying to do this thing all over again, and there are other women out there that he's been with that might ruin this for us."

Willow patted my knee. "Then, don't let them ruin it for you."

Luna nodded. "Yeah, don't let some random stranger who may have entered Will's life at some point in time ruin what's blossoming between you two."

Willow smiled. "That, you have control over."

Even though I knew deep in the pit of my soul that Will was a different person than the boy I knew back in high school, I still felt just as lost as the day I found those pictures of him kissing other girls on his social media account. I leaned back against my chair and puffed out my cheeks with a heavy sigh as the girls leaned back in their own seats. With food and drinks in front of us that we hadn't even touched, I let my eyes fall closed.

Then, Luna's voice sounded to my left. "All right, this is supposed to be girls' time. So, no more tears."

Willow's voice came from my right. "She's got a point. We've got food and drinks and blankets."

Luna giggled. "And a massive mounted flatscreen."

My eyes eased open. "You guys thinking what I'm thinking?"

Luna and Willow answered together. "Movie time."

The three of us leaped out of our seats and gathered up everything from the table. We bussed it over to the living room before we flopped down onto the couch, with me in between my two best friends. Luna grabbed the remote control and started fishing around for a movie marathon on television while Willow divvied out blankets.

And as Luna settled on a Hallmark romantic comedy marathon, I felt Willow staring at me.

"Yes?" I asked.

Willow tucked a strand of hair behind my ear. "Promise me that you'll talk to Will tomorrow. Okay?"

I nodded. "I promise."

Luna settled back against the cushions. "Then, the three of us can get together for dinner tomorrow night and talk about how things went."

I smiled. "I like the sound of that."

Willow squeezed my knee. "Everything is going to be okay. All right?"

And while I knew in the pit of my gut that I'd come out just fine on the other side, that revelation didn't stop it from hurting. It didn't stop me from being worried, or panicking, or generally feeling as if the world were crumbling around me. But, as I sipped my lemonade and hunkered down for a Saturday movie marathon, I thanked my stars that Will had to go into the office today.

I simply hoped he didn't have to work tomorrow so we could finally get this resolved.

So I could finally get some rest.

So I could finally be at peace.

❦ 22 ❦

Will

I jumped at the resonating 'slap!' that crashed against my desk. I gazed down at what looked like an email, and it wasn't until I read it that I realized what it was.

"I don't need to read it. I sent it," I murmured.

Bryce planted his finger in the middle of the email. "That'll be three."

I sighed. "Three what?"

"Three fucking business trips you've shoved off onto me without even asking, Will."

I leaned back in my seat. "I thought you liked the business trips?"

"Yeah, sure! But, not three in a fucking row. We always tag-team this stuff, you know that."

I leaned my head back. "Can you get to the point? I've got a long day ahead of me."

He swiveled my chair around and planted both hands on either side of me before gazing heatedly at my face.

"You love these business trips, and Bart needs your help more than ever right now with what he's trying to pull off."

I patted his cheek. "You know you're better suited for that kind of shit."

He smacked my hand away. "You love the perks that come with these trips. The dinners and the parties and the glad-handing. You practically get off on it."

"Thanks? I think."

His eye twitched. "So, spill."

"Spill what?"

He snickered. "Spill why the hell you're all of a sudden shouldering me with all of these trips without so much as a head's up. I've got a family, you know. Two kids and a--."

I glared at him. "Yeah, well, I've got a family of my own coming along, and they need me just as much."

I felt him studying my face, and I closed my eyes. "I'm not that easy to read, Bryce."

"What in the world do you mean, 'you've got a family of your own coming'?"

I finally met his eyes. "I should be a little bit easier to read now that I've dropped that bomb."

He narrowed his eyes. "Something's happened with Sadie since she moved in, hasn't it? And for some reason, now you feel you can't leave her. How close am I?"

I wanted to shove him away, but I resisted the urge. "I'm in a lot of trouble here, and I've got no idea what the hell I'm supposed to be doing."

Bryce cocked his head. "Oh, shit."

I pointed to a chair in the corner. "Have a seat."

He wasted no time in pulling it up to me and sitting down. "When did you find out?"

"Remember the doctor's appointment when we moved Sadie in?"

His jaw hit the floor. "You're fucking with me."

I shook my head. "No. I'm not. She just hasn't said anything to anyone yet, I don't think. And I want to respect that."

He slowly nodded his head. "Can you even bring yourself to say it? Because let me tell you something, Will, you can't even begin to move forward until you can say it out loud."

"I honestly don't know if I can."

I sat there staring at my brother that all but knew the truth. And as my mind raced with so many different things at once, I struggled to find a volleying point to begin the long, endless strings of worries and issues that had cropped up since Sadie and I figured out we were pregnant.

"Dude, can you hear me?" Bryce asked.

I snickered. "Of course, I can hear you."

"Then, tell me what I just said."

I blinked. "You said something?"

He sighed. "Will, this is serious. Have you and Sadie talked about this at all?"

"Not... particularly? She's just kind of been keeping to herself."

"What, and you've been letting her?"

I furrowed my brow. "What the fuck am I supposed to do? I can't make Sadie do something she doesn't want to do."

"Yeah, but you can go in there and be a man for her."

I leaped to my feet. "That's exactly what I've been doing. Feeding those animals day in and day out. Cooking, cleaning, giving her as much space as she needs."

He pointed as he stayed seated. "That last one. That's a bad decision."

"Why!? Why is that so bad?"

"Because right now is the worst time for her to feel like she's alone."

I fell back into my seat. "You know what's happened between us. I want her to come to me. I don't want to have to force myself onto her."

"Trust me, she's come to you already. She's pregnant, for crying out loud. That's about as 'coming to you' as it gets."

I grinned. "No pun intended?"

"Shut up and focus."

I cleared my throat. "Right, right."

He leaned forward. "Look, everyone deals with stress differently. You? You crack jokes. You get people laughing. That's how you deflect. But, not everyone copes that way. Have you ever thought that Sadie's method of coping is withdrawing from the world?"

I paused. "So, she's not creating distance with me?"

He shook his head. "No. She's creating distance because she's stressed. Just like you are. And do you really feel like being alone right now?"

Holy shit. "No. I don't."

Bryce settled his hand on my knee. "Say it out loud."

I licked my lips. "Bryce, I--."

"Say it, Will."

I felt myself inwardly fighting with this. I mean, it wasn't like Bryce didn't already put the pieces together. So, what was the harm in saying it out loud? Then again, if Sadie hadn't told anyone yet and she figured out I said something to Bryce-- which would ultimately get back to Willow--what then?

Would I fuck things up like I had last time?

"You can't tell a soul that you know," I whispered.

Bryce nodded. "My lips are sealed."

"Including Willow."

"Trust me, this also means Willow."

Yet still, my lips wouldn't budge.

"Will, it takes a village to raise a child. And in order to create a village, you have to talk. You guys are going to need help, and that help needed to start the second you two figured out what the hell was going on."

My eyes danced between his. "What if I say something and she leaves? Like last time?"

He took my hand. "Dude, last time you made out with three girls at a drunken frat party and put that shit online. This time? You're announcing something precious and sacred, and filled with love. Because I know you love her,

Will. I see it all over your face every time you two are together."

I held his hand tightly. "Bryce?"

"Yeah?"

I swallowed hard. "Sadie and I are pregnant."

He nodded slowly. "So, that vasectomy of yours that you boasted about for weeks didn't take."

"And now you understand why I'm so worried."

He sighed. "Please tell me you didn't fuck all of those women without protection. Please tell me you weren't that stupid."

I shook my head. "Not a fat chance in hell. I'm not an idiot. STD's are still a thing. But, what if one of the condoms burst? Or failed, somehow? What if Sadie and I really try our hand at this family thing before some woman pops up, claiming her child is mine as well?"

He released my hand. "Did you ever stop to think that Sadie isn't stupid and probably has those same worries too?"

My eyes lined with tears, and I quickly blinked them back. But, Bryce had already seen them.

"Have I ever told you how petrified I was when Pat told me she was pregnant?"

I shook my head mindlessly. "No."

"So, I haven't told you that I was equally as petrified when Willow told me she was pregnant?"

That caught my attention. "What?"

He chuckled as he leaned back in his chair. "Yeah. I'm serious. I was fucking scared out of my mind."

I blinked. "Why were you scared when you were with her? I thought you already knew you loved her when that happened?"

He shrugged. "Has loving Sadie helped you at all with how scared you are right now?"

"I mean, I understand being scared with your ex, Lucifer, but Willow?"

He barked with laughter. "Dude, children change everything. And I mean, absolutely everything. Your life is no longer going to matter because you are going to reframe it with the idea of protecting this helpless little thing you're going to be holding in your arms in a few months. And trust me, there's no feeling like it on earth. Until you gaze into your child's eyes for the very first time? You've got no idea what love is; or dedication, for that matter. You'll never understand the lengths you're willing to go to for your woman until you watch her grow with your child."

"So... what does that have to do with being afraid?"

He grinned. "I was scared with Pat because we weren't supposed to be anything but a one-night relief of stress. But, with Willow? I knew it meant dedicating myself to her for the rest of my life. I knew it meant protecting her and providing for her for the rest of my days, because that's what I wanted to do. It links you to someone forever. I'll always be linked to Pat through our daughter, and I'll always be linked to Willow through the child we've had together. Never underestimate how absolutely petrifying it is when you first realize you've gotten someone pregnant. Because as someone who's got multiple kids? It doesn't get any less scary the second time around."

I felt relief wash through my veins, even though I had so many other questions I wanted to ask him. I mean, what was childbirth like? What would Sadie go through after we had our kid? What are the appropriate things to put in a nursery? Did we even need a nursery?

"Can I ask you a few--?"

A knock came at my office door before the doorknob turned, and I saw Bart standing there. The door swung open and revealed wide eyes and a slack jaw that told me everything I needed to know.

So, I waved Bart into the room, and he quickly stepped in before closing the door.

"Holy shit, Will," Bart said breathlessly.

I puffed out my cheeks with a sigh. "How long have you been standing there?"

Bart stared me down. "Long enough."

I folded my arms over my chest. "You've never visited the Rocking R Ranch this much since we took over the family business, but now I see you in my office two or three times in the span of a couple of weeks? What gives on your end?"

He chuckled. "What can I say? The family gossip is getting juicy, and I've always been a sucker for a nice dose of drama."

I rolled my eyes. "Asshole."

Bart smiled. "Plus, I haven't decided yet if we will have enough room in our Houston office once the refinery project kicks into gear. So, I'm making sure I explore all of my options."

Bryce nodded softly. "Well, this office space isn't big enough for the three of us. And your temporary space over beside the front door won't get it either."

I licked my lips. "Do we have any open rooms down there at the stables by any chance?"

Bart clicked his tongue. "Yeah, no. I'd never be able to actually get any work done with the horses right there waiting for me to saddle them up and take off to the practice ring."

I pointed at Bryce. "Then how's that deal to buy that old bank building coming along? What's the update on that?"

Bryce drew in a deep breath. "I'm still jumping through a few hoops, the owner is interested, but no contract yet. At least, it's one of our options."

I looked up at Bart. "Well, let's keep our fingers crossed. If we can snag that old bank building downtown here in Conroe, it won't take but a couple of months to gut it and set up the bare bones. The three of us could work out of our new head-quarters right here in town along with the additional staff we'll be hiring." I shrugged. "If everything goes as planned with the refinery project, that is."

Bryce paused. "What would we use these offices for, then?"

Bart grinned. "This would be more or less overflow office space...set up a big office for Dad of some kind. You know, some kind of an honorary thing. And let's not forget about

Uncle Ryan. He'll be moving back to town when and if the refinery project comes to fruition."

I held up my hand. "And since when did Uncle Ryan decide he wanted to move back to Conroe?"

Bryce smiled widely. "When you decided to shove the second Houston trip off into my lap. It was during that meeting. Anyway, we need more help around here. And Uncle Ryan? He *is* Dad's baby brother, you know? I think down deep he's tired of the big city of San Antonio."

Bart nodded. "Yeah, it was at that meeting you missed, Will."

I narrowed my eyes. "And you're just now telling me?"

Bryce rubbed the back of his neck. "Yeah, since you've been off on cloud-nine with the Sadie thing for the last few weeks. Now can we get back to what we were talking about before Bart walked in."

I sighed. "Fine, fine. Get a chair from somewhere and pull it up."

Bart simply walked over to me and perched on the edge of my desk. "Whatever decision you make, I'm going to stand by you. Okay?"

I patted his leg. "I appreciate it."

Bryce scooted closer to us. "That goes for Sadie, too, because she's family now. Even if you two don't work things out and just do the co-parenting thing."

I scoffed. "Oh, we're making it work. It's just a matter of getting over this hump."

Bryce clicked his tongue. "Hate to break it to you, but the hump is never over."

My head fell back. "Wonderful."

Bart patted my shoulder. "Just listen to your gut. It's going to tell you what to do."

As I closed my eyes, I felt overcome with so many emotions. Pain and worry. Happiness and joy. Fulfillment and affirmation, as if I'd finally reached a point in my life I wasn't sure I'd ever reach. But, one of the emotions ringing true to, my heart rang out louder than the rest.

I'm head over heels in love with Sadie.

And I knew I'd do anything necessary to keep our family together and provide for her and our child the best life possible.

Come hell or high water.

❦ 23 ❦

Sadie

Of course, Will had to go into work today as well. Something about making up for a business trip or something like that. Honestly? I only heard part of what he said this morning when he walked into my room and kissed my forehead. And while it was a wonderful way to wake up, sort of, I had been burning holes in the hardwood floor as I passed back and forth all day.

Waiting for him to come home so we could talk.

Once I heard his truck pull up, though, I stopped. I held my breath as his door closed. As he walked up the front steps. Even as he jiggled the doorknob. I listened as he pressed the key into the lock and turned, easing the door open with a coolness that would've gone unnoticed had I not been intensely staring at the door.

And when Will's face came into view, he grinned.

"Miss me?" he asked.

I held my hand out toward the kitchen table. "Can we talk?"

His grin faltered. "Uh, oh."

"No, no, no. No 'uh oh's. Just... just a talk."

He slowly made his way for the table. "All right. Want to tell me what it's about?"

I sat in tandem with him, my eyes never once deviating from his face. But, when I gazed into Will's eyes, I could tell he was excited about something.

"What?" I asked.

He blinked. "What what?"

I snickered. "What are you so excited about?"

He chuckled. "You know, I always thought I was harder to read than this."

I shook my head. "You've always been easy to read. Out of all the words I'd use to describe you, 'mysterious' isn't one of them."

"Thanks? I think?"

I giggled. "So, spill. What are you so excited about?"

He shook his head. "Oh, no, no-no. You're very somber right now. You have me worried. What's on your mind? What do you want to talk about?"

"If you have happy news, we should start with that."

"Aaaaaand, now I'm officially very worried."

I sighed. "I didn't mean it like that."

He took my hand. "Sadie, what's going on?"

I looked down at our connection. "Before I say anything, I just want to be upfront with the fact that the reason why I'm asking is because I want to come at this issue from every angle. I want to be able to look at this situation from a perspective as to how this is going to affect our child. Okay?"

I saw a shadow of a grin tick his cheek. "I think I know what you're about to ask."

I felt my face pale. "You do?"

He nodded. "But, it's important that you get the chance to say it. So, say it. Whenever you're ready."

I drew in a deep breath before I started rambling. "Okay. Here it goes: I know I'm not the only woman you've been with since your vasectomy. That's a simple fact. And while I know you're here with me now, and you're going to tell me 'that's all that should matter' and all that mess, that's not all that matters. Because I'm pregnant, and we have a child on the way. So, we need a contingency plan for what happens if we try to do this thing together, and some woman comes out of the woodworks after we try to be this happy little family and make the claim that her child is *also* yours."

His thumb stroked my skin. "Is that all?"

I swallowed hard. "Huh?"

He scooted his chair closer. "Is that all that's on your mind? Because if it isn't, I want you to get it all out right now. Just dump it."

I felt my stomach turning into knots as silence fell

between us. This was how he was reacting to what I had to say? It took me by surprise. Part of me expected him to be frustrated. Another part of me expected him to be upset. And even still, another part of me expected him to cast me out onto the street after insinuating such a thing. But, all he did was sit there and give me a platform to continue talking.

Only, I didn't have anything else to say. "I, uh..."

Will sat patiently. "It's okay if you don't. I just want to make sure we don't leave any stone unturned before we make this an equal exchange."

I narrowed my eyes. "Who are you, and what have you done to my Will?"

He smiled gently. "Your Will. I like the sound of that."

I blushed. "I mean, technically, you are?"

"You did have me first."

I smiled. "I did, didn't I?"

He leaned forward. "And they are moments that I'll never forget. That's the difference, Sadie. All of those other women? They were forgettable. A balm to soothe an ache in my soul that I had no idea how to fix. But, you? My first love? The woman currently carrying my child? You're worlds away from them. You're the stars in my sky and the sun in my daytime. I can't even recall their names, but I can recall every feature of every crevice of your body that my lips have kissed."

My blush deepened. "William."

He chuckled. "It's true, Sadie. And I'm here to tell you that whatever happens--if that *is* something that happens--you and I will tackle it together. As a team. As a couple."

"But, if you've gotten someone else pregnant, then how--?"

He nodded. "If that does come to fruition, then I need to step up. I need to do what's right by the child out there that I don't know I've got yet. It's only fair, and it's a responsibility I have to take, especially since it was a risk I didn't even know I was taking. But, if it happens, I need you to know something."

I gazed into his eyes. "What is it?"

He leaned so close to me that I felt his breath against my lips. "I need you to know that I love you. And that's never going to change."

I held my breath. "You what?"

He slid his hand behind my head as if to cradle me. "I love you, Sadie. I've never loved anyone the way that I love you. And there isn't a day that's gone by since things happened between us all those years ago that ever made me stop. Even after we broke up back in college, the only thing I ever did was try my hardest to fill the hole in my heart that was left because of my mistakes."

I felt my eyes welling with tears, and I parted my lips to tell him the same thing. Only, his finger pressed against my lips, as if to silence me.

And with his finger still, there, he continued. "You are everything to me, Sadie. You are every dream and every piece of encouragement and every ray of sunshine that falls from the skies. You make me want to be better. Period. You make me want to be good. Period. And no, I didn't plan on having children after I saw what Bryce went through with Patricia.

No, I didn't see my life taking this kind of a turn. But now that we're here, I wouldn't trade it for all the wealth or sanity or women or treasures in the world."

A tear slipped down my cheek as the full effect of his words blanketed my heart. I saw the sincerity behind his eyes. I felt the impact of his words in my soul. My heart skipped so many beats I thought I might drop dead as my mind replayed his confession over and over, like a movie reel I kept rewinding.

I can't wait to tell the girls.

His finger slid from my lips, and his smile grew from ear to ear. His forehead touched down against my own as my eyes fluttered closed, my nose drawing in his scent. His arms wrapped around me. He pulled me into his lap. And as I threw my legs over his and snaked my arms around his body, I placed my cheek against his shoulder.

"I love you too, Will."

He chuckled softly as he peppered my forehead with kisses. But, I didn't want that kind of a kiss. I tilted my head up toward him as his lips came down for yet another soft kiss, and I captured his mouth with my own.

Causing him to pull me even closer against his body.

My hand slid through his hair as he dipped me back, causing me to giggle against his lips. Our tongues fell together in a familiar tango that sent shivers up and down my spine. I felt alive in his embrace. His head tilted off to the side as he kissed me deeper, allowing me a taste of his wondrous presence. And as he picked me up in his arms, hovering me in midair, still-life images popped up in my head.

Me, in a beautiful white wedding gown.

Will, in a gorgeous white tuxedo.

Us, trying our best to put together a crib.

Me, rubbing lotion on my massive stomach.

Will, bringing me breakfast in bed with our child in a carrier against his chest.

I saw our entire life unfold before my very eyes as I felt my body descending against something soft. And it wasn't until he finally broke our kiss that I cupped his cheek.

"I promised the girls I'd meet them for dinner to tell them how this talk went."

His hand crept up my inner thigh. "Then, let's really give you a story to tell them."

I giggled as his lips fell to my neck. "I'm going to be late. I don't have time."

He growled against my skin. "When do you have to leave?"

I tried to focus as he suckled my skin. "Uh, told them I'd meet them--oh."

"Focus, beautiful. What time?"

I groaned in frustration. "Seven. Seven, seven, seven."

"Where at?"

I gasped. "Cafe in town."

His hand cupped my heated pussy. "So, a fifteen, twenty-minute drive?"

I nodded my head quickly. "Uh-huh, uh-huh."

He kissed down my clothed breasts. "So, assuming time for--mm, beautiful--getting ready. Even if it takes you forty-five minutes to put yourself together, you still wouldn't have had to leave for another hour after that."

A shiver shook my core. "Oh, Will."

I felt him unbuttoning my pants. "And that gives us sixty entire minutes to really get you ready for a shower."

I sighed. "Oh, William."

He slid my pants off my body. "You're beautiful, Sadie. An absolute vision. And I can't wait to watch you change and morph with our child."

I shot up from the bed and quickly got up onto my knees. I watched as he ripped his shirt over his head, so I mimicked his movements. And the second my bra slid down my arms, he crashed his lips against mine.

Sending us hurtling back to the mattress.

Our bodies bounced as his cock pressed hard against my clothed pussy. Somehow, my bra made it to the floor before Will cupped my breast and lapped against my puckered peaks. I felt on top of the world as his hands explored me. His teeth bit down softly, causing me to whimper as my back arched against his naked muscles.

"Will, holy shit," I hissed.

He grunted. "I'm going to make the best use of this hour. And if I do my job, right? The girls will know exactly how this talk went just by how you're walking."

I giggled. "I dare you."

With a growl, I felt him rip my panties clear off my body.

A sensation that brought just as much pain as pleasure. I panted as his hands rushed up my legs, massaging my thighs open. I parted my legs for him as he laid down against the bed. He slid them over his shoulders as his fingertips parted my wet pussy lips. My hands flew into his hair. I prepared myself for the onslaught of his tongue as my entire body contracted. Waiting for that very first lick.

But instead, he kissed my lips softly. Over, and over, and over again.

He sighed. "Damn it, you smell amazing."

I massaged his scalp. "You're just amazing, in general."

He kissed the dollop of excess on the top of my inner thigh. "I really do love you, Sadie."

I smiled up at the ceiling. "And I really do love you, Will."

Then, as our profession hung heavily in the air above our naked bodies, I felt his tongue fall against my clit.

Licking and swirling, until my body quaked against his face.

24

Will

I buried my face into her beautiful warmth and felt it trickle all the way to the bottoms of my feet. My heart soared through the heavens as I lapped at her pussy, feeling her shiver and buck. I wrapped my arms beneath her thighs and pulled her closer to me. I might as well have put up a tent because I had no plans to go anywhere anytime soon.

I wanted to drink her down until she begged me to stop.

"Will. Holy fuck. Oh, my God."

I grinned. "Whenever you're ready, so am I."

She gripped my hair tightly. "Don't stop, don't stop, don't stop."

I swirled the tip of my tongue around her pulsing nub as I slid one hand back to the front of her body. As her legs clamped around my cheeks, I teased her entrance with the tip of my pointer finger. She groaned as my finger breached her body, slowly filling her as it slid against her juicy wet walls. But, it wasn't until I inserted a second finger that the most unearthly, most amazing sound tore from the back of her throat.

"Oh, my Gooooood."

I crooked my fingers and flattened my tongue against her slit, allowing her to use me as she pleased. She pulled me closer and bucked hard against my body, quickly unraveling as my tongue stroked. I felt her walls clamping down onto my fingers. I felt her walls quivering at my assault. I teased her and taunted her with nothing but my mouth until she was a helpless glob of putty in my hands.

And when she popped, my palm filled with her arousal.

"Holy fuck, William!"

Her nails raked against my scalp as I dug my tongue deeper into her pussy. I lapped furiously, feeling her shake and groan as her body backed up. I followed her, movement for movement until I had her pinned against the headboard. Her hands flew from my hair, and I looked up with my eyes, watching her tightened peaks jump for my viewing pleasure.

Then suddenly, her legs fell away from my face.

Just as her palms planted into the headboard.

I grinned as she used the leverage she had to buck furiously against my face. I felt her juices dripping down my chin, and it made my cock pulse against the sheets. I wanted her. I needed her. For the rest of my life, this is how I wanted us to be. Wrapped up in each other and so in love, we simply couldn't stand it.

This is the woman I want for the rest of my life.

"I'm coming again. I'm coming again. Will--I--it--oh, shit!"

I growled against her pussy as her second orgasm washed over her. But all too soon, I felt her hands against my forehead.

"No, no, no, no. I can't. Not anymore. Please, Will. It hurts so good."

I slowed down my lapping and made sure I drank every single drop of her down. And as I kissed her swollen, sensitive mound, I eased my fingers out. Her walls were thick with need, and her juices dripped everywhere, coating and marking every surface it could touch. It was an honor to watch her pour out for me, both physically and emotionally.

And I promised myself at that moment never to take it for granted.

The moment didn't last long, though. Not with her commanding hands. And the second I felt her grip in my tendrils again, she pulled my body on top of hers. Our lips collided, and she licked herself off me. An action that started my cock weeping with need for her. I fell between her shaking legs, exhausted from their efforts, and as I lined myself up with her entrance, I gazed into her eyes.

"I love you," I whispered.

She cupped my cheeks. "I love you, too."

Effortlessly, she let me in, and I quickly pinned her wrists above her head. I pounded against her, watching her reddened body jump for me as her face contorted with pleasure. I couldn't get enough of her. I'd never had enough of her. Her walls, clamping around my dick. Her sounds blanketing my ears. Her body, giving me a soft place to land as the beast inside me finally rattled free.

"I'll never have enough of you," I growled.

I released her wrists and fell against her, rutting like a wild fucking animal. Her arms wrapped around me tightly, and I sat back onto my haunches, bringing her form with me. With my cock still sheathed in her warmth and my arms tightly around her waist, I slid from the bed and walked us toward the wall on my shaking legs.

Only to pin her there and thrust against her.

"Oh, Will," she groaned.

I panted against her neck. "I love you. You're fucking perfect."

She gasped. "I've missed you. I've missed you so much."

I threaded our fingers together. "You'll never have to miss me again. Never, Sadie. I promise you that."

I pinned her hands against the wall as my eyes found hers. I slowed my movements, swiveling my hips, and watching the sweet torture wash over her face. I peppered her bare shoulder with kisses. I sucked patches of skin against her neck between my teeth. I didn't stop until she was properly marked with hickies I knew the girls would ask about.

Then, our movements fell into sync.

With every thrust, she bucked. With every swivel, she rolled. I breathed the air she afforded me with every kiss she allowed me to have, and I lost myself in the beautiful universe of her soul. I felt as if we were moving as one. Two pieces that had been disconnected for so long, finally reunited.

Almost as if no time had slipped by at all.

"Will, I'm so close."

I pumped a bit faster. "Hang in there. I'm coming with you."

"Will. Please. I-I-I--."

I grunted. "Just... a little more."

"Will!"

"Come with me, Sadie!"

"Holy fuck!"

I filled her one last time before I unraveled, my balls pulling up into my body. I felt her quaking against me as her pussy milked my dick for all it had to offer. And oh, I gave her everything. Thread after thread of hot arousal burst from deep within me, bringing with it an animalistic sound that could only be described as feral.

The room undulated and spun around me as my orgasm crashed over me.

And when Sadie collapsed in my arms, I plummeted to the floor. Taking her with me before I settled her in my lap.

With my dick dripping of her fluids.

"Holy shit," she whispered.

I kissed her temple, lazily. "My thoughts exactly."

She panted softly. "I'm going to need two showers after that."

I chuckled breathlessly. "Then, I can take one of those with you."

She giggled. "If we do that, I'll definitely be late."

"Would it be such a terrible thing, though?"

She looked up at me. "For the girls? Yes."

I sighed playfully. "All right, all right. I guess I can give you up for an evening. But do something for me?"

"Anything."

"Lay in bed with me for a bit?"

The beautiful smile she graced me with filled me with enough energy to pick her up. I collapsed with her in my arms onto the bed and felt her wiggle against me, trying to nuzzle as close as she could. With her face pressed against my neck and my arm wrapped around her waist, I allowed myself to think about how good it would feel to wake up every morning with her in my arms.

But, just as I went to ask about living arrangements, she beat me to the punch.

"This feels nice," Sadie said softly.

I kissed the top of her head. "You could have it every morning if you wanted it."

She kissed my neck softly. "Well, maybe that's something we can arrange, then."

"We could make the guest bedroom the nursery if we did that."

She nodded softly. "We could, yes."

"But, even if we didn't do that, I'd still want you in here with me."

She raised her eyes to meet mine. "I'd still want to be in here with you, too."

I smiled. "That settles it, then. Tomorrow, I'm going to take a half-day with work and get you moved in before I head to the office."

"Are you sure? We could always--."

I stopped her counter-offer with a kiss. A sweet, delicate kiss that still managed to make me feel like the most powerful man on the planet.

"I said what I said," I murmured.

She giggled. "Well, fine then."

I kissed her forehead. "There's always the option of having you moved in by the time you get back from dinner, though."

"And had you actually let me speak, you would've known that I had that exact thing on my mind."

I chuckled. "All right. I won't stop you with kisses every time you have a counter-opinion then. Deal?"

She kissed the tip of my nose. "Deal. Though, I hope you don't use that tactic during negotiations with your business. I'd hate for the father of my child to be kissing other dudes because they don't agree with him."

I barked with laughter. "What makes you think they're all dudes?"

She playfully glared at me. "Better that than the alternative."

I cupped her cheek. "There is no one else but you."

"I was only kidding, Will."

I stroked my thumb against her skin. "Still. I want you to

look at me and know that I'm serious. There is no one else in my life, but you. There's no one else for me, but you. You're stuck with me, girl."

She swatted my chest. "Don't ever say that again. It sounds so weird coming from you."

I smiled. "Whatever you want, my dude."

She fell apart in laughter, and I couldn't help but join. Hearing her laughter fill my cabin took this place from a simple abode I dwelled into an actual home. I felt at home in this place whenever Sadie was with me. And simple touches like sharing coffee with her in the morning and listening to her laugh only solidified what I wanted out of my life.

Her, at my side.

For the rest of it.

Sadie kissed my lips softly, pulling me from my trance. "All right, I need to go take a shower."

I kissed her a little deeper. "Sure I can't change your mind?"

She pressed her hands against my chest. "Will."

I sighed dramatically. "All right, all right. Tell the girls I said 'hello.'"

"I'll be back before you know it, handsome."

I clutched my heart. "I don't know how I'll go on without you."

She padded into the bathroom. "Drama, queen!"

I shot up from the bed. "Hey. That's drama king to you!"

"All right, *girl!*"

As I laid in bed laughing to myself as the shower turned

on, I sighed with content. For the first time in all the years of my life, I sighed with relief, with happiness, instead of stress. This was all I needed in my world. Sadie, this cabin, our child, and her animals. Even if the family business tanked tomorrow and I had to completely redo our financial responsibilities--even if I had to hop back into the job market--so long as I had those four things I knew I'd be just fine.

"I did it," I whispered to myself.

I couldn't believe I actually had it. A family, like Bryce. Love like my parents had. A home, like we all had growing up as brothers. Were there risks involved? Sure. But, every wonderful thing in life came with a great risk. That much I knew. Whether it was the business, or watching Bryce with his children or even taking care of the animals, it all came with a certain amount of risk.

And the risk here was *definitely* worth the reward.

I laid there until the shower turned off, and the bathroom door ripped itself open. Steam poured out and cloaked the bedroom in a soft, warm haze as Sadie padded around the room. I sat up and watched as she held a towel tightly against her body. I watched her hips sway beneath the soft microfiber as she walked down the hallway towards her room. A room she'd only occupy for a few more minutes before she left.

Because once she went to go have dinner with the girls, I was moving everything.

"Will?" she called out.

I swung my legs over the edge of the bed. "Everything okay?"

She gasped. "Will!"

My eyes widened as I leaped up from the bed. Her squeal sent me charging out the door and down the hallway until I rounded the corner into the guestroom. My heart leaped into my throat. I felt the air charged with electricity as my eyes darted around for Sadie.

"Where are you!?" I called out.

Then, I saw her march out from the corner, where her body had been blocked by dressers and opened doors and shadows.

"Look at these hickies you left on my neck!" she squealed.

I blinked. "Wait, that's it?"

"What do you mean, that's it!? I'm about to go have dinner. You knew that. It'll take me at least twenty minutes to cover these things."

"So, you're not hurt? You're okay?"

She paused. "Oh, goodness. I'm so sorry. I didn't mean to worry you."

I walked over to her and tucked a strand of wet hair behind her ear. "I'm always going to worry about you. It comes with the territory. You just... you made that sound, and everything bad ran through my mind all at once."

She cupped my hand and kissed my palm. "I'm sorry. I didn't mean to do that. But, I mean, look at these damn things. You look like you mauled me."

I grinned. "And you loved every second of it, don't even play."

She smirked. "Maybe. But now I'm really going to be late. Seriously. It's going to take me forever to cover these up."

I shrugged. "Or it's a chilly night, so you can wear a scarf."

She paused. "Is it really a chilly night?"

"It could be if you simply blamed it on the pregnancy. Do the girls know?"

Her eye twitched. "Would you be upset if they knew?"

"That depends."

"On?"

"If you'd be upset that my brothers know."

She smiled. "Not one bit."

I smiled back. "Then, neither am I."

EPILOGUE

Sadie
Seven Months Later

With my legs spread toward a fan wafting up my thighs and the fabric of my dress hiked up over my stomach, I slathered shea butter lotion all over my stretch marks. My skin itched constantly, and it felt like my body wouldn't ever stop growing. I mean, every time I thought it couldn't possibly get any bigger, it did!

I guess that's what happens when someone has twins.

As my palm mindlessly rubbed the butter around, I watched out the window as Will fed the animals. With the feed sack tossed over his back, I saw the veins of his forearms popping with each cup of food he tossed into the buckets by the south side of the storage barn. I hadn't been able to feed the animals for a few weeks now. I simply couldn't bend over without one of our children jamming their feet into my lungs. And even then, I still insisted on pulling my weight around the house.

Until the doctor put me on bed rest.

Premature bleeding was no joke, but apparently very common at this point with twins. And Will has definitely kept up with the doctor's orders in the strictest sense. He didn't let me cook, or do the slightest bit of cleaning. He even used the doctor's orders as an excuse to get into the shower with me at random moments just to wash me down and condition my hair.

Though, I didn't mind that part much.

I waved out the window as Will waved at me from outside, then I felt my stomach jump. My hand quickly fell to my gut as I grunted in pain, doubling over with my feet planted against the floor. Even though I smiled from ear to ear, that didn't stop my hips from aching. It didn't stop my pelvis from crying out for mercy.

And it didn't stop Will barreling through the front door.

"Sadie, are you okay?"

He dropped to his knees in front of me as I reached for his hand.

"Come here. Come here," I said breathlessly.

And when I placed his hand against my exposed stomach, both of our children kicked at once. Sending me into a frenzy of pain as Will pressed his lips against my stomach.

"I love you guys so much. I know you're in there. Hello

there. It's Daddy. Hi."

I leaned back against the couch as he peppered my skin with kisses and riled our kids up so much with his voice that I thought they'd take me to my grave. Nevertheless, I didn't stop him. I tried to enjoy the moment as much as I could because I knew once the kids were here, the pain wouldn't matter. None of the bleeding, or the shock, or the doctor's appointments, or the sheer nausea of their kicks would matter once I had them in my arms.

And the best part? I was the only woman bearing Will's children.

That's right. Even after we went public with our relationship around town, no one came forward with babies claiming they were Will's. Which was the biggest relief of all, for both of us? And while we had our rocky moments just like any couple, he'd been steadfast and loyal for all of us. He was my rock. My source of comfort. My sweet place to fall and the one person I felt expressing every emotion with, no matter how silly it felt.

And I had the honor of being that for him as well.

Especially with work constantly getting in the way of things.

"Can I get you anything? Are you thirsty?" Will asked.

I smiled. "Actually, I could use some of that limeade. That last batch you made was amazing."

He chuckled. "And I just happen to have one last big glass for you sitting in the fridge."

"Ugh, you're amazing."

He kissed my forehead. "And you're spectacular."

Will had been wonderful in putting his life on hold for our family. He temporarily pulled out of competing in the local rodeos and halted all of his business trips to Houston for the foreseeable future. I mean, he video conferenced in as much as he could from the kitchen table, but other than that work stayed in his office.

Which was a blessing in and of itself.

"How are things with the bank going, sweetheart?"

I heard Will sigh. "It keeps getting postponed, like always."

"Do you think you guys should look at another place for the company's headquarters?"

He sat down next to me and held out a glass. "No, something in my gut tells me we need to stick with this move. Besides, Bart's still struggling to find a place to purchase to install the petroleum refinery, so until that's locked down, there's no point in moving people from Houston to Conroe without jobs for them to take."

I took a long pull of the limeade. "Oh, man, this is fantastic. And you make a good point."

He held up his own glass. "I also make a good limeade."

I clinked my glass against his. "The best."

He grinned. "You're the best."

"Awwww, I thought you'd never admit it."

He chuckled as he took my hand, and together we stared out the window. As we watched my animals frolic around in the front and side yard, my thoughts fell to Luna. I wondered how she was doing with everything that had happened recently. I mean, her two best friends were essentially down and out because of pregnancies and family stuff, and Luna was battling hell on earth with her father.

"You heard from Luna lately?" Will asked.

I snickered. "Sometimes, I think you can read my mind."

"Sometimes, I wonder why you're still questioning it."

I giggled, but it quickly faded. "I'm worried about her, Will."

He squeezed my hand. "Want me to invite her over for dinner or something? I can make myself scarce."

I shook my head. "No. She's bunking with her father for a little while longer. They had to go back into his left hip and remove a bone spur that was apparently inhibiting his rehabilitation."

He hissed. "Ooooh, that sounds like shit."

"Tell me about it."

"Well, what are her favorite kinds of things? We could send her a 'forget everything around you for a second' basket."

I looked up at him. "Have I ever told you how amazing you are?"

He winked. "Only every day."

My face fell. "Not every day. Let's not toot that horn too much."

"What? You don't like my horn? Because I'm pretty sure my horn is what got us into this situation."

I swatted at him playfully as he fell apart in laughter.

"Anywaaaay, how are the animals? Have they been given you any trouble?" I asked.

His laughter died down. "Nope. They're all doing well. Oh! I did get a phone call from Betsy up the road. She said Highlight will be delivered tomorrow evening."

My ears perked up. "Well, it's about damn time! She's postponed delivering that miniature horse to me for days now!"

"I thought that might bring a smile to your face."

I threw back the rest of my limeade. "Oh, man. I can't wait to get out there with--."

"Sadie," he warned.

"I mean after I give birth. I'm not that stupid."

"You sure? Because just last week you were trying t--."

I held my finger up. "Uh, uh, uh! I'm turning over a new leaf."

He murmured beneath his breath. "For the fifth time."

"I heard that."

"I love you."

I smirked. "Yeah, yeah, yeah."

He threaded his arm behind my back. "How are you feeling? You need anything else?"

I tilted my head back to look up into his eyes. "I have everything I need right here on this couch with me."

He smiled brightly. "You craving anything in particular today?"

"Actually, no. I'm not."

"You sure?"

I paused. "Why?"

He leaned his lips down to my ear. "Because I've got some leftover fruit in the fridge that needs to be... blended."

My eyes fluttered close. "Please tell me there's more--."

"Passionfruit? Oh, there's definitely more passionfruit."

My stomach growled with hunger. "Could I have another smoothie bowl?"

He kissed the shell of my ear. "Coming right up, beautiful."

As he pushed himself off the couch, I reached for the lotion and rubbed some into my stomach one more time. The fan against my gigantic thighs felt absolutely amazing, even though we were still in the throes of winter. It didn't matter, though. All that mattered was Will's happiness and the health and safety of our kids.

Everything else was for the birds.

"Does Luna like chocolate?" Will called out from the kitchen.

I slid my dress back over my stomach. "Oh, yes. Especially that nasty chocolate with orange flavors? Oh, she loves that stuff."

He chuckled. "Not a fan, I take it?"

"Ew, no. Have you had those chocolate orange ball things? They taste like chalk and regret."

He barked with laughter. "I'll make sure to get you a dozen of them for Christmas."

I groaned. "That's worse than coal."

A smoothie bowl appeared in front of me. "Here you are, gorgeous."

I settled it right onto my stomach. "I'm going to miss my little table once the kids are here."

He kissed the top of my head. "We could always make more."

I gripped the spoon. "Let's focus on these two first, then we can see what happens."

He kissed my head again. "Whatever you want, beautiful."

I looked down at my smoothie bowl to dig in and take a massive bite. But, something shiny caught my gaze. I put my spoon down and studied the shimmering raspberries on top, wondering how in the world Will got them to glitter like that.

However, as I poked at them with my spoon, I heard something tink.

And that's not the kind of sound raspberries make when touched.

"Hey, Will!?" I called out.

He sat down beside me. "I didn't leave."

"Oh. Sorry. Uh, why do the raspberries sound..."

I touched them again with my spoon, only this time the raspberry fell away. And just behind it, sitting on a small foundation of neatly-stacked sliced strawberries, was the most gorgeous cushion-cut diamond ring I'd ever seen in my life.

I was in such shock that I almost didn't pick it up.

So, Will did the honors for me.

"Sadie?" he asked.

I kept my eyes on the ring between his fingers. "Yeah?"

He crooked his finger beneath my chin and raised my gaze to his. "There you are."

My eyes welled with tears. "Will?"

I watched as he slid to both of his knees on the floor, perched right at my stomach.

"Sadie, you are my world. And not only that, but you're about to give me another world I could have never dreamt of for me."

I gasped. "Oh, my God. This is happening."

He smiled as brightly as I'd ever seen. "I love you. That goes without saying. But, I need you to know that I'd die for you, Sadie. If someone walked into this cabin right now and pointed a gun at you, I'd hop in front of that bullet every single time. You're more precious to me than my own life. And that will never change."

A tear streaked my cheek. "Oh, my God."

He chuckled. "I hope that's not all you can say."

"Yes!"

"I haven't asked yet."

My face fell. "Then ask, jerk-face."

He snickered. "So aggressive sometimes."

"Will."

He got up and sat beside me on the couch again. "Sadie?"

I gazed into his eyes. "Yeah?"

"Will you marry me?"

I nodded my head softly. "Yes. Oh, yes, Will. I will so, so, *so* marry you."

The two of us couldn't stop giggling like little school children as he picked up my left hand. But, when he went to slide the ring onto my finger, it wouldn't go past my second knuckle.

"Fucking water weight," I murmured.

He snorted. "Here. Let's do this."

He reached around my neck and unclasped the beautiful white gold locket he'd gotten me for my birthday a couple of months ago. I watched as he slid the beautiful, twinkling diamond ring onto the delicate chain. He fastened it back around my neck. I fingered the ring softly before I opened the locket, smiling down at the picture of Will's handsome face.

And I knew just what picture to put on the other side of the locket.

Us and our children.

"It's perfect," I whispered.

He cupped my cheek. "You're perfect."

I raised my gaze to meet his. "No, no. This time? You're the perfect one."

He slid his fingers through my hair before he cupped the back of my head. "Any life you want, Sadie, I'll make sure it's yours. If you want a new ranch house just like Bryce and Willow for our football team of kids? Then, so be it."

I giggled. "I don't think I can give you a football team. But, maybe a starting line-up for soccer?"

He chuckled. "I'm also going to build you a barn. A massive barn... bigger than any barn you could have ever imagined for yourself. I want there to be enough space for the animals you have now, and any new ones you accrue in the future, as well as their food and tack."

"All I want is you. The rest? I don't care about."

"I care, Sadie. And I want you to have these things. It's necessary for you to have some sort of a barn anyway. I'd like to build it for you. Will you let me?"

"Of course, I'll let you. You know that."

His palm slid down to my neck. "Just promise me something."

"I've already promised you my life and my future. What more could you want?"

He grinned. "Cheeky, cheeky."

"What would you like me to promise, handsome?"

"I want you to promise that if you ever have second thoughts--if you ever feel like you can't--."

I leaned forward and stopped his words with a kiss. Not because I didn't want to hear them, but because I knew it would never happen. There would never come a moment in my life where I'd regret Will. There'd never come a point in my walk with him that I'd no longer want to be at his side. So, I didn't even want to breathe it into the air. I didn't even want the universe getting a *hint* that something like that was possible.

And after my lips lingered against his, our foreheads touched.

"Don't even speak it," I whispered.

He brushed his knuckles against my skin. "Always be open with me. That's all I ask."

I captured his lips softly once more. "You never need to ask, because that's already a given."

I felt the ring settling in my prominent cleavage, and I couldn't wait to tell the girls. I mean, they'd go absolutely bonkers over it. But, apparently, Will had the same kind of idea, because before I knew it my phone was in my lap and he was urging me to video call the girls.

So, I did.

"Girl, let me tell you, this damn molar tooth this baby is cutting is about to put me in my grave. I'm not sleeping one bit," Willow said.

Luna popped up on the screen. "You think that's bad? Try dealing with an over-the-hill, grump-ass, traditionalist of a man that can't have his nightly beer because it mixes with his pain medication. Oh, and my ex called. I didn't pick up, though."

Willow's face fell. "You didn't call him back, did you?"

Luna scoffed. "Not a fat chance in hell. He's a jerk, and I blocked his number just to prove a point."

"You go, girl. It's about time you got rid of his begging ass."

I smiled. "Life is grand for me."

Willow gawked. "What!? No pregnancy bitching or last-minute regrets or sleepless nights?"

Luna squinted her eyes. "What's that around your neck?"

I picked up the ring. "Oh, this old thing? Just a present Will got for me."

Willow paused. "When did Will get it for you?"

Luna gawked. "No."

I nodded. "Yes."

Luna shot up from her desk. "No, he didn't!"

Willow shrieked with happiness. "Bryce! Bryce! Will did it! He proposed! Get your ass over here!"

I fell apart in laughter as Will flopped down onto the couch beside me. Bryce rushed the video chat and gawked over the ring, just like the girls did.

"Oh, my God. You have to let me help you plan this. We could have a wedding here at the ranch!" Willow squealed.

Luna nodded. "I agree. An outdoor wedding would be wonderful, especially with the beautiful backdrop of the ranch."

Willow kept rattling on. "We can get you through your pregnancy, maybe wait until the twins are at least three months old. Then, we can plan for a fall wedding when the trees are changing colors, and then we can babysit while you guys go on your honeymoon!"

Will leaned into the picture. "Hi. Future husband here would like some input, too."

Luna cocked her head. "What? You want an open beer bar or something?"

Will licked his lips. "Actually, a fall wedding wouldn't be half bad. We would make the colors a nice, rich rust red, maybe silver as well. Line it all with a nice golden yellow and really do it up with a western, barn-hosted reception."

Willow blinked. "Who are you, and what have you done with Will?"

I barked with laughter. "If you can fight him for the position of wedding planner, then go for it."

Luna held up her hands. "I know when to surrender. I'm not dumb."

Willow smiled. "Yeah, well, I've still got some ideas floating around that I'd like to bounce off you guys. Will? You up for dinner sometime this week?"

I scoffed. "And what am I? Chopped liver?"

Willow clicked her tongue. "Girl, you know you're coming."

Will chuckled. "Make sure to have some limeade around. She can't get enough of the stuff."

Bryce yelled from the background. "I made a nice limeade slushie!"

Willow's voice fell to a whisper. "He really does."

I licked my lips. "Sign me up."

Luna sighed with content. "It's going to be a fun spring on the Rocking R Ranch next year, you guys."

I looked over at Will, and he kissed my lips softly, almost as if he'd been waiting for me to turn. A gesture that made me giggle against his lips. Every once in awhile, I grew overwhelmed with how quickly things were moving. Then, there were moments like this where I didn't want it any other way.

"Two more months," I murmured.

He grinned down at me. "Two more months."

And honestly?

Life couldn't get any better than this.

Follow Luna and Bart's story in Cowboy's Fake Girlfriend.

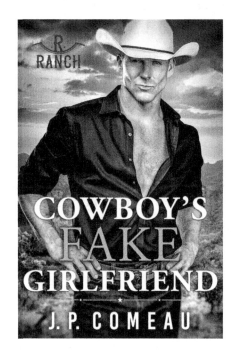